ST. MARTIN'S PAPERBACKS TITLES BY

# RELENTLESS AARON

# Seems Like You're Ready

RELENTLESS AARON

St. Martin's Paperbacks

This is a work of fiction. All of the characters, organizations, and events portrayed in this novel are either products of the author's imagination or are used fictitiously.

Relentless Aaron, Relentless Content, and Relentless are trademarks of Relentless Content, Inc.

SEEMS LIKE YOU'RE READY

Copyright © 2004 by Relentless Aaron.

Cover photo © Shirley Green

All rights reserved.

For information address St. Martin's Press, 175 Fifth Avenue, New York, NY 10010.

ISBN: 0-312-94963-4
EAN: 978-0-312-94963-1

Printed in the United States of America

Relentless Content, Inc. edition / July 2004
St. Martin's Paperbacks edition / October 2008

St. Martin's Paperbacks are published by St. Martin's Press, 175 Fifth Avenue, New York, NY 10010.

10 9 8 7 6 5 4 3 2 1

# Special Dedications

**W**ell, here we are, so many books later, so many dreams fulfilled, and still there's a burning desire to do more, to achieve greater, and to inspire a generation of hungry minds. Charge it to my passion for excellence, my willingness to make sacrifices, and the courage to own up to my mistakes. But then, to do that, you must look deeper than the stories; you must go deep into the mind of a man who is unwavering in his drive to succeed. You must decipher the energy that is necessary to get the job done, and you must do so with great understanding, compassion, and the want to gain wisdom.

**T**o see what makes Relentless Aaron, you must know that a burning desire coupled with the most sincere work ethic, and then sweetened with the audacity to take major risks, can then become a goal achieved. In some shape, form, or fashion, Tiny Wood, Emory Jones, Steven Juliano, Paulette Gilmore, Julie & Wataani, Carol & Brenda, Earl Cox, Renee McRae, Tanisha Waller, Curtis Southerland, Rick Gunter, Pete Oakley, Shetalia Miller, Henry Perkins, Alise Jackson, Makeda Smith, Mechel Miller, Courtney Carreras, Diane Littrell, and Anthony Butler all extended their unconditional support that permitted me the license to achieve what only I imagined, and what only I could bring into existence. It is because of these people that I walk the walk, run the race, and live among the stars.

**S**uper thanks to all of the hundreds of thousands of sharp, savvy, devoted readers whom I've met (in prison and out, on the streets or in the bookstores, from all across the world), who chose to lend me their time, knowing that it would not be taken for granted and that I would indeed deliver to them the absolute best stories ever told.

My Sincere Thanks to You All!

*Relentless Aaron*

*To the children I've sired, taught, nurtured, and raised,*
*I'm inspired by you.*

*Love, Dad*

# Chapter 1
## DOUGLASS

I learned very little about the grandparents on my father's side of the family. And even less about Grandpa then Grandma. But I do recall some of my younger years, and those occasions when I was dropped off at their house up on Battle Hill in White Plains. The place was ghetto fabulous with the funky air battling it out with the kitchen odors. In the end, both the kitchen and foul air settled into the deep shag carpet.

Babysitting me wasn't hard. Just get me in front of that old record player and leave me with the stack of Jackson Five records that myself and other grandchildren would play over and over, despite the cracks or scratches in the vinyl.

*Just a little bit of love every day*
*will surely keep the doctor away.*

I used to play that damned "Fly Robin Fly" 45 so much that I don't think I'll ever forget the lyrics. I will also never forget seeing a shotgun in Grandma's house, behind the door in her bedroom. I was incredibly curious in my adolescent years, but not enough to touch *that* thing. Instead, I was more interested in

Grandma's entrepreneurial spirit. She grew her very own greeting card store—a small shop on Prospect Avenue in Mt. Vernon, New York—from the bottom up. When she passed away, my father took it over. He in turn took her efforts a step further, molding the small enterprise into a candy store, and eventually, the entrepreneur stepped his game up and developed a chain of six bodegas.

For some reason, I got to know my grandparents on my mother's side of the family a lot better. Grandpa was the only relative I've known to represent the Indian heritage in our blood. He looked the part too, with the long, stringy hair and deeply wrinkled Coppertone skin. And, in my eyes, he also carried himself as a traditional Indian; always so reserved, sitting quietly while watching TV or reading a book. My grandmother meanwhile was the irritation, the energy, the voice, and the love that Grandpa enjoyed to death.

Out of all my relatives, Grandma probably made the biggest impression. I remember those 6-ounce glasses of apple cider she served me, just like I remember those greasy foods Dad used to sell in the deli. Grandma was also on the radical side of feisty. In a humorous way, she was sarcastic, pessimistic, disbelieving, and very set in her ways. These attributes were inherited by my mom, and are subsequently a part of me, her only son. My mother wasn't the complacent type to just sit around the house and mope about my father's frequent absences or constant infidelities. Absolutely not. What that did was set the tone for the conflicts, the debates, the arguing, and the domestic violence that took place at home. Dad needed a woman to take care of him, put up with him, and still maintain her dignity while keeping her fucking mouth shut. And that was *not* Mom. Mom rebelled. She was Miss Individuality. Already so versatile in her youth, Mom was always involved in the arts and music, and she was even a hockey player in school.

Even as my parents hooked up and made enough babies to keep Mom busy, Mom's wants and desires and progressive nature stood out like a flag or a symbol of her independence and liberation. I wouldn't lie and say ours was a single-parent household, but with Dad always working, it felt just like one. It was only because of Mom's curiosity that my childhood was more of a pretty picture; she made sure I was exposed to a brighter and more prosperous lifestyle than the hood we were subjected to.

**D**igging into the family heirlooms, I found the newspaper clippings showing Dad as the next Jackie Robinson before he lost his leg during a car accident. The follow-up press clippings showed how he overcame the odds by bouncing back, despite his prosthetic limb. There was significant pain in that closet—put away, filed in boxes, out of plain view. It was a history that I would not come to terms with until years later when I'd shed my youth and ignorance.

I only remember the good times, and the family joys up until maybe age nine or ten. I remember getting to know my two sisters as they came into the world one by one. Mom would have her three children do exercises regularly and we'd stand on line for a tablespoon of castor oil. I remember Christmas when it was rich and plentiful; the fire engine under the tree, the homemade ornaments, and the two or three snowfalls so massive that cars couldn't budge through our suburban streets. I remember spending quality time in a tree house I built in our backyard, and how me and my sisters would tease the neighbor's dog, until the day he broke loose and chased us. Those were the days.

In my early teens the joys I knew as a youngster gave way to more miserable circumstances. Dad took some risks, investing heavily in bullet-proof glass and the expansion of the deli. Yet even though the new deli and liquor combination was the biggest business in our neighborhood, the venture did not come without its challenges. In short, the family business began to suffer growing pains. There were financial woes and certain sacrifices had to be made, including Dad selling our first home, with our family of four forced to downsize our living arrangements to squeeze into a small apartment positioned over one of his stores. That meant sleeping side by side with my sisters and doing what was necessary to make the family unit work. And I never realized how heavy the burden, to be just one man with so much potential, with so many duties, and with so many expectations to fulfill. However, my dad always survived the rain and maintained his want and desire for more. I later learned about the other brothers I had, children my father sired out of wedlock. I also learned of the other women—women other than my mom. Couple that with Dad's growing gambling habit and the pieces of the picture begin to come together.

Dad's other life was a secret to all of us, until later on. And I'm not sure if my mother was aware, but it must've taxed our family unity somethin' vicious. Not to mention the expense of carrying other women and children, and how that must've contributed to the downsizing from a four-bedroom house in the suburbs to a two-bedroom apartment in the ghetto.

Still, the "family businesses" once again flourished, especially with the heavy markups on the groceries, as well as the fast food and liquor that was available for consumption twenty-four hours a day, seven days a week. It was a sign of the times, and the one significant entity that my father decided to keep blossomed in the spring and bloomed during the summer. The deli and liquor store combination was a hit, serving customers for blocks in every direction. As a family, we survived the employee thefts, the armed robberies, and my dad's infidelity, and I personally survived the neighborhood shenanigans that I began to indulge in—stealing bikes, gambling, and various degrees of trespassing. We eventually moved back to the north side of town, back to the suburban side of Mt. Vernon's four square miles of mostly residential properties.

All the while, even as Dad battled to achieve success with his small business, enjoying a positive cash flow from the sales of the other stores, as well as (I'm sure) his new fifteen-hour-plus distance from his family, I still maintained this mischievous lifestyle that brought about constant school troubles, neighborhood conflicts, and frequent whippings from both Mom and Dad. I remember Mom's whippings and how she used switches until the bushes where we lived lost their consistency. Dad, on the other hand, played a whole different ball game, wielding a leather belt that was my worst enemy. Or maybe *I* was my own worst enemy and the belt was merely the fix-it for my troublesome ways. I'm not sure why I never changed, why I never made the effort to "straighten up and fly right," as Dad always used to say while he beat me until I had welts on my body, and sometimes until I bled. But when I think of it now, it seems like it was a mix of my being the punching bag for that black man's burdens, and me waiting to chart my own course, do what I wanted to do, and take whatever I could get my greedy hands on along the way.

I went through a puberty that was hardly recognizable; no significant, overnight voice changes like I remembered from Peter Brady, the TV character that I most identified with. And I didn't experience any obvious physical growth. Just a gradual growth that left me lanky and hyperactive. But that was no major issue, not for the dysfunctional life that I was leading.

My big wake-up call was hearing my parents' arguments escalate to physical abuse. With all three children in the house and my smallest sister hiding under her bed, my dad would slam closed his bedroom door and he would put the belt on Mom, no gentler than he put it on me. I listened to the leather hit her skin and I knew how it felt. I knew how bad it stung. I knew it hurt like hell and I knew it left marks. And Mom had light skin, so her marks were more prominent.

I'd hear Mom scrambling through the bedroom, running as best she could from Dad, trying to escape through the door. Screaming. Crying, *"No!"*

I wondered if all of Lorraine Avenue could hear this as I heard it. And I began to weigh things and compare all that was happening behind our closed doors to the various other ills on our block. Maybe our block being a "dead end" had some significance because just as violence existed in our house, it also went on across the street, where an Italian family lived, as well as in another home where a family of Jamaicans lived. During my lengthy relationship with one of the girls from that family, I found out that the lady of that house was getting the dog shit beaten out of her. In a sick way, seeing other dysfunctional families and knowing of their experiences with physical abuse made it seem okay. Still, these images are etched into my mind like a sad Billie Holliday tune with words I'll never forget. They are images I must live with for the rest of my life.

I guess I'm jaded.

# Chapter 2
## ANGEL

**S**ometimes I swear I am stuck on stupid, to have let things get so out of hand so quickly. I should know better, really. Because my success didn't come overnight. I worked long and hard hours on and off the set, in and out of the studio, for it. Frankly, I gave up most of my childhood for it. But when success comes, I don't think *anybody's* ready for it because it comes so suddenly—like a typhoon hitting. I'm *still* spinning years later.

Like, I honestly can't think of one bad thing in my life, except for my periods. They make me feel icky. So nasty. Whenever I'm onstage now, I have to look down to see if there's a spot forming between my legs. And here I go again—spoiled, because I'm thinking I should be special: *Why couldn't God make it easier on female celebrities?* Like, maybe he could make it so we menstruate one day a month. And give us a specific time or at least let *us* set an appointment. *Seriously*. This way we can work around *his* schedule, or hers if we're talkin' about Mother Nature.

Well, since it's gotta be this way, Mother makes sure I always have plenty of black pants in my wardrobe. It's a good thing I can afford such luxuries 'cause back in the day we had nothin'. We might as well have been trailer park residents. My father was a door-to-door salesman sellin' shoes. Shoes! Imagine that! Didn't someone tell him that there're, like, shoe stores galore on every main street and in every mall across America? If you ask me, goin' door-to-door went out with the rotary telephone. It's a wonder me and my brother, Tray, got to eat at all. While my father was usually out knockin' on doors, doin' his best to avoid dogs and stuff, gettin' doors slammed in his face, sometimes I think of the days he must've come home with a real check—that would be for *way* less than Tray was makin' on his newspaper route.

Mother was an LPN. But LPNs make less than registered nurses, so Mother did stuff like cleaning up after white folks. For some of 'em she had to be there when they ate and wait 'til the food passed through their body and into the bedpan. Nasty job, but somebody had to do it. I just wish it didn't have to be *my* mother.

After paying the rent and the smaller bills Mother would pay for my acting lessons, my dance classes, and my vocal coach. I didn't get to go out and play, like most other kids in San Diego. No movies or trips to the San Diego Zoo or to the amusement park. I was always either getting ready for an audition, going to an audition, or coming back home from one. Of course, I'm like, happy about all of it now. 'Cause I wouldn't be who I am today without all that experience. Without the sacrifices, talent shows, beauty pageants, singing in front of the family at our reunions and stuff, I know things would be much different. But (no disrespect to Mother) I think she was livin' her dream through me. One time I was about to take a trip to Opryland—somewhere down south—and I got sick. I think it was the flu or something. Well, instead of staying home, Mother loaded me up as usual and on the blasted Greyhound bus— we didn't have a car—she hurried to get me better. Of course it didn't work, so I was sick as a dog at the audition. I did my best anyway. I sang "Cabaret," which is my favorite song by Liza Minnelli. I nailed it. They hired me.

However, the gig lasted only about a month. Even though I killed it at the audition and joined the company, Mother realized that there wouldn't be enough money to pay for our back and forth trips to Nashville, not to mention the hotels and stuff. So I quit Opryland and we decided to stick to auditions back home in the local areas, like San Francisco and Los Angeles. I stuck to the "Cabaret" act. Time after time folks couldn't believe a li'l black girl could do a classic piece like *that* so well. I did the French version perfect too. Sometimes I'm amazed how blessed I am.

When I reached age ten Mother seemed desperate to get me to Hollywood, to New York . . . to anywhere but home. With time I had a few projects under my belt; I came a long way since that Huggies commercial I was in as a toddler. There was the Nestles commercial, the Toys "R" Us commercial, and I must've done a dozen public service announcements for the State Library Association. I wish I read as much as I *said* I read. I couldn't tell if those folks at the Ad Council loved me for me or because I did the commercials for free. Mother says either way it's all good exposure—nationwide television. So I guess it's all right.

Then, just when I was getting tired of the PSAs, Mother got a call from my agent. They wanted me for a pilot. Some show with an older comedienne as the headliner. I made the first cut. The second cut was scary, 'cause there were girls there who were really big. One we have all seen on *Cosby*, another from *Sesame Street,* and another who I know for a fact had done more commercials than I had. *Well,* I figured, *go for it, Angelica.* And I did. It took every bit of ghetto attitude I had in me to get the part, but I got it! My first sitcom. *Mama's House* lasted for three seasons. I played Angelique (the writers for the show wrote a variation of my name into the script so I'd feel comfortable) and they paid me $1,000 per show. Including the regular season and a few holiday specials, I can remember doing about fifty shows. After paying my SAG dues, taxes, lawyers, agent fees, and minor expenses, I came home with about half of that. Mother talked Dad into moving to Los Angeles; she convinced him that it was *my* town—hence the name Angelica. It was a new me once we moved. I got my hair braided and my tits started filling my bra. My agent would make sure I was seen at all the hot events. The Emmys, the Grammys, and the Oscars. At the American Music Awards I met Mr. Dick Clark. My agent says in Hollywood, he's next after God. Mr. Clark told me he heard my singing on one of the holiday specials of *Mama's House* and that I had a future as a recording artist.

"A performing artist? Singing?" I asked. "Are you *kidding me?*"

With his pearly white teeth glowing in my face he said, *"Whitney Houston had better look out!"*

I almost lost it when Mr. Clark said that, because Whitney's my *girl.* I *bow* to Whitney. I know all of her songs word for word.

**S**o my agent is goin' out of his mind pushing that idea of recording an album to my mother. Before I know it, he's got me hooked up with Jingle, a producer who had a top ten song on the charts. Jingle is cool. Down to earth. Even though he's a good friend of Quincy Jones's son, he keeps it real with me.

He told me straight up, "Angel, drop the valley-girl talk. You're about to be the biggest thing to hit the planet since french fries."

So I had to try and take words out of my vocabulary. It's a little hard 'cause like . . . *aww, there I go again.* I'm supposed to think of eating dead rats every time I say *like* and *okay.* It actually works.

Anyway, Jingle says he's molding me to be the "it girl." And we worked for weeks on some songs he wrote. Mother didn't want me to do this one song called "For Me," because of one of the lines in the song:

*I didn't know it before,*
*when you came through the door,*
*who knew I could have*
*so much more . . . for me.*

Mother says it's too provocative 'cause I was only fourteen at the time. She would get an attitude, saying, "Who's coming through my baby's door?" And "How much more of what is she gonna have?"

And I'm thinking, *Mother! It's not like I don't know what goes where.* So Jingle gave me something special, this song called "Like That." It goes:

*I was always like that,*
*the one who thought about you,*
*the one who thought you were cool,*
*the one who watched you in school . . .*
*I was always like that,*
*always the best I could be*
*so one day you will see*
*that there's nobody like me.*

The music behind the lyrics was the hottest that R&B has heard in a long time; some hip-hop beats under Linda Ronstadt's "You're No Good" hook. It was dreamy, mysterious, and hype all in one song. Jingle leaked the track to some of his buddies at KJLH radio and it became the most requested record for eleven straight weeks. Things have not been the same since. We rushed to complete a full album for Artistic Records, because they wanted to make sure that I was not just a "one-hit wonder" before they invested the big money in me. Then there was that one meeting. It was like my whole life had been laid out on the table in front of a whole heap of white executives. My work in commercials and on *Mama's House*, and about a thousand different photos from my fourteen years of professional work were right there on that big conference table. My mother, who was also my manager, my agent, my lawyer, and Jingle were all there. After a whole bunch of talk about advances, points, tour support, marketing budgets, and artist development, they played a video reel. It was a two-minute blitz of my television appearances, some home activities, and me and Jingle in the studio.

All the while, my single "Like That" is playing as the theme music for the promo. When the lights came back on everyone stood and applauded. I cried boo-hoo tears while the others shook hands and made the deal of a lifetime. No more scrimpin' and savin'. No more running out of money and out of the back doors of motel rooms. No more cheap clothes or sample sales because we *had* to. If there was anything I *had* to do from that point on, it had to include singing and (as my agent says) flashing my intoxicating smile.

# Chapter 3
## DOUGLASS

**W**hile so many other people were likely going through life's tough times, I was living a life to die for by my twenties. Instead of struggling to pay rent, or a car note, or any other significant bill, I was instead feeding into one of those idiosyncrasies I have: appreciating the fine, mint dental floss as opposed to the heavier grade. It's like a romance I have every now and again, or some type of obsessive-compulsive disorder. There I was running late for a big audition I put together, and instead of stressing or concerning myself with how things might go and what problems I might face, I was enjoying my dental floss. Just something to know about me, and my ways.

This was just a moment I was having as I plucked another speck of that funky, odorous grime onto the mirror in front of me. I had to stop for a minute and stare at myself, knowing that if there wasn't so much anticipation bubbling up inside of me, I probably wouldn't be all pressed up against the bathroom mirror like I was, with less than five minutes to spare. Maybe it was just my intuition, but I had to get this flossin' done *just in case*. You never know, there might just be some kissin' goin' down later.

It was Saturday morning. Luther Vandross's "Stop to Love" was pumping over my Pioneer sound system in the bedroom, and filtering through various small and large speakers that I had strategically positioned in the front and rear of my crib. I lived on the ground floor of a split-level colonial. The way it's set up, it appears as two residences. My side faces North Avenue. My father's side has a prestigious columned entrance, which faces a side street and a pair of lakes out in front of New Rochelle High School. The oval driveway cuts through the front of this corner property and there's enough grass around the home to play miniature golf. This is how the late '80's embraced me—with luxury, convenience, and curious scrutiny from those who never got a good look inside my life. Dad and Mom had long since divorced. She moved to Grandma's (Grandma had moved from White Plains to California years ago), and my father took advantage of a lease-option deal I stumbled upon in New Rochelle.

The house we lived in was awesome. It had about twenty-five rooms, and three of New Rochelle's landmarks—the twin lakes, the high school, and the statute of Thomas Payne—were just across the street. And although I was geographically close to Dad, I hardly saw him during the space of a week. If not for a priority here and there, we'd have little else to talk about. Family or not, there was still so much pain in our past. The leather-belt whippings, the infidelity, and his overall direction in life was a great burden to bear. He never made time for me since "work" always required his presence. The result was the two of us, the last of the Mohicans, being left to fend for ourselves, focused on whatever life brought our way. For Dad, it was keeping time with the bar he started running after he sold the deli and liquor business. And for me there was my cable TV show, my live talent shows, and the assistance I gave him to promote his business. For my input, I'd get $500 a week, and of course I was living rent-free in this humungous house fit for a king. This was an all-expenses-paid way of life that allowed me to experiment in free enterprise—and to taste-test any woman I wanted.

In the meantime, most of my days and nights were filled with music, usually playing at high volumes and with no certain consistency. It could be rock, jazz, hip-hop, or soul. It could be folk, classical, or the old Broadway musicals. I hate talking in the morning. *Hate it.* It's just a zone I assume, a mental silence that I've grown accustomed to. It is a mood not to be questioned, but also one that I sometimes break away from thanks to some euphoria or high or other unknown joy. And yet, this still follows a night of incredible dreams come true, or fanatical fantasies—and nothing but nothing can follow up, or overwhelm that. So this mood I have most mornings is something like the morning-after-sex syndrome: *"Don't touch me."* Except with me, it's *"Don't talk to me."* This morning the volume of my music was particularly obnoxious; enough to support my argument, and for me to get my point across without discussion.

"Rain, get yo' ass up! We're supposed to be at Marty's and Lenny's by ten."

"I *am* up!" she responded in kind, then said, "I gotta get your son ready—bottles 'n stuff."

*Hmmm. All of a sudden it's my son because she wants an excuse for being late.*

I stepped out of the bathroom and into the bedroom to see her pulling up some skintight leotard. Her dress for the day had already been laid out on the chair the night before, prepared for the image she needed to maintain in public. Today was a big rehearsal for our premiere of *SuperStar*, a new cable-access TV show that would showcase the best in amateur talent. In the past two years I'd produced more than a hundred of these types of TV shows for average amateur performers. We promoted the talent, the performer's families paid to see them, and the venture took off. Now in our fourth season of these one-hour weekly television shows, it was time to break free from *The Westchester Talent Show*. It was time to adjust with the times. Time for *SuperStar.* No more hokey-pokey, local-yocal talent, with banjos, tap dancing, and violin players. This was a new jack world, and R&B and hip-hop dominated every major chart and, in some cases, threatened the future of rock & roll.

And here was Rain, my latest girlfriend. It was a relationship that "stuck," thanks to her submissive nature and the no-contest presence she introduced me to. All sucked in by her energy, her youth, and her perky breasts, I fell hard for Rain. More than just the mother of my first son, more than a convenient body for freaky sex, Rain also performed the duties and the unconditional labor that helped to drive and nurture my various entertainment ventures. I eventually made her a codirector for the cable TV show and for the live performances we produced. To keep it real, outside of Rain being born from parents who didn't care, and adopted and raised by parents who did, I basically *made* that girl. I saved her life. *Captain Save-a-ho rides again!* Because of me she wasn't considering suicide anymore. I romanced her and courted her, and I let her know that she *was* wanted and desired. And the moment she got comfortable, I ran up in her—served her ass raw-dawg. Nine months later she had Douglass Jr. I also gave her dancer-wannabe ass a title with the talent show to keep her content and accessible. Being her boss gave me the power to shut her up, turn her up, flip her over, and make her jump whenever I said the word. And, truth be told, she didn't mind that *one bit.*

So for her to come out of her face like this—talkin' about "I *am* up"—was out of order. And then her response changed to a plea—*but quick.*

"I'll only be a minute," she whined.

"Aiight, Rain. I'm tellin' you, I'm outta here in five minutes. Sink or swim! Five minutes!" I barked.

I heard her suck her teeth at me, and I knew she was feeling that military pressure as she leaned into Dougie Jr.'s crib to pick him up. But I just let her be as she spun around with the infant, laid him on the bed, and proceeded to change his diaper. While I finished getting myself dressed, Rain rushed around with a pout, grabbing baby bottles, diapers, and a bag to carry it all. Still, she wasn't fully dressed herself. I had a feeling that no matter what she did, however quickly she did it, there was no way she would be ready in time as I demanded. But I was hoping as much, because I wanted her to realize this morning that I meant what I said. She should've gotten up earlier.

Eventually, good sense must've told Rain to look outside, because I was already behind the steering wheel, revving up my black Chevy Caprice like a loud warning. Just in time, Rain snatched open the passenger-side door.

"What's wrong with you, Doug? Can't you wait another minute?" She was distressed, and her Camay brown skin turned red.

"I *told* you five minutes. Five means *five*. Did you think I was jokin'? You think this is a *game*?"

Rain seemed at a loss for words, caught between the baby inside the house and my ruthless attitude outside.

"Whaddaya want *me* to do?"

"Are you ready now?"

"No! I told you I gotta make the baby's milk. I don't even have my sneakers on."

"Then take a cab. Now close my door." And boy did she ever. She slammed it so hard the car even rocked a little, and I could feel the pressure against my eardrums. Man, if she woulda broke my window, I swear I woulda busted her yellow ass. But with my unspoken threat, I sped off. I quickly forgot her and focused on the day ahead. Just as I cleared the driveway, I could see she slammed the front door to the house, too. I swear that woman is a pain in my ass.

# Chapter 4
## ANGEL

**W**hile my career in entertainment seemed to be growing in leaps and bounds, I was taking a lot of days off from school. Eventually I got a tutor. Norma would teach me math and English in the mornings and social studies and history in the afternoons. If there was a day that I had to be on the set, Norma would come and we'd work between segments. Since I didn't have such a tremendous part in the sitcom, I spent a lot of time in my dressing room. Hotels and dressing rooms are my second homes. And once *Mama's House* was taken off the air, Mother decided to keep Norma, and I did my sixth, seventh, and eighth grade studies at home. When ninth grade came around I begged my parents to let me go to public high school. I just wanted to be normal, like the other kids. My father was all for it, but my mother gave all kinds of excuses about stalkers and bullies and peer pressure. Sometimes she gets on my last nerve.

Eventually, they gave in and I ended up in the 3-I program, a special group within L.A. Central High that allowed certain students to arrange their class schedules based on their own personal agendas. So really, I was spending just a few hours a day in school.

Sometimes classes started in the early morning, other times I'd have an evening class here and there. It worked out well enough that I could both pursue my career and still fulfill my educational obligations. And that's probably because I loved school and learning so much. Plus, I got a lotta love from other students, who treated me like the school celebrity. But I couldn't stop the haters from doin' what they do best. Not that I was all stuck-up or anything like that. I had gotten involved with school activities as much as I could. Mother joined the PTA. And I even sang in the school choir—no matter how boring the songs were. For the most part I'm glad to have gone through the challenge of public school. It definitely impacted me. And when the prom came around, I savored every second like a strawberry milkshake. I wish I could say this was a normal experience. But there's no way. I was Cinderella—*for real*. One of the new superstar NBA ballers actually stepped to my father and asked if he could be my prom date. I almost died, 'cause everybody knows Lefty is the next Jordan. And he was smart to talk to my father instead of my mother because he *stays* in front of the TV when the ball games are on.

To top that off, Father calls me in the den while Lefty's there and says, "Lefty just asked if I minded you two going to the prom together. It sounds like a good idea to me, babycakes. How about it?"

And I'm like, "Dad! Why don't you just baste me with honey and butter and give the guy a fork and napkin? For God's sake!" But of course I said *yes*! But dang, just when I thought I was in for one of those famous crossover moves he does on the court, there was nothing happening. Lefty was the perfect gentleman.

I thought, *Am I gonna be a virgin forever?* But at least I got the stretch limo treatment, the flowers, and a beautiful diamond tennis bracelet. How could I go wrong?

While that first date wasn't the eye-opening experience I hoped it would be, it was, at least, some breathing room from under the watchful eyes of Mother. It was my chance to spread my wings, if only for a little while.

My homeboy Rory had been my so-called boyfriend at the time. But sometimes I wondered if he even counted in my bigger picture. He was like the boy next door. My father gave him "the speech" a long time ago, so he never really tried anything. Never made a pass. And if he had, I probably would've felt funny about it, as long as he's been around.

He's more like a brother than a boyfriend. There were no juicy kisses or quick feels. It left me somewhere between committed and deprived. Not that I knew what I was missing. All I had to go on for sexy romance scenes in my life was made-for-TV movies, and the stuff I watched on soaps and cable reality shows. But watching it and doing it were two entirely different things.

Jingle and I finally completed the album for Artistic Records and the nationwide promotional tour began. I must've visited every radio station and TV show that existed. Some places like Atlanta, Washington, Chicago, Detroit, Florida, the Carolinas, and the entire New York region—where I did three and four, sometimes five, radio shows in the morning, racing from one to the other—were chaotic. Then we'd revisit the same stations in the afternoon and evenings. The same old questions again and again. I got so friggin' tired of hearing "So tell us, how did you get started? How does it feel to be a celebrity? Which do you like more, TV acting or singing?" Then, of course, every program director, radio personality, and marketing and promotions person wanted to take photos with me, which I didn't mind.

After the photos I'd spend a couple of minutes doing "drops" for the station.

"*Hi! This is Angel and you're listening to blah-blah-blah on W-blah-blah-blah, the hottest, greatest, most fabulous station in the nation . . .*" I'm sure I did enough kissing up to make you wanna puke. Mother was along for the promo tour, and she would do her best to keep me sharp. She wanted me to approach each station as if it was the first and only on my tour. I was suddenly pigeonholed as the new child star on the block. Nickelodeon, Disney, and *Sesame Street* kept me real busy with all their TV shows and live events. But it's a living and I just love performing for kids. Plus, I never imagined I'd be signing autographs like this. The kids make me feel like *I'm* Whitney Houston. During these shows I began to run into other performers more and more frequently. They always told me how they liked my work and how cute I was with my braids and all. Why I always gotta be *cute*? Shoot, I was fifteen already; couldn't I be sexy or at least a knockout? Cute sounds so . . . so childlike.

Sincere thought I "looked good." And he said so,

too. It woke me up to where I really started checkin'
for him more and more. He sings with NUBIAN
and does most of the tenor parts in the quartet. Their
songs are infectious—like, everybody listens to
them. Everyone says NUBIAN reminds them of The
Temptations and The Four Tops. But I didn't know
too much about them until I saw them on the repeats
of the *Motown 25* special. They have all the right
moves, the outfits, and their voices are heavenly. I
ran into Sincere again at the Soul Train Awards—
NUBIAN won best R&B group that year—and that's
when he dropped the "you look good" line on me. It
made me shiver. 'Cause NUBIAN got all kinds of
women screamin' for them, but Sincere noticed *me*.
We exchanged phone numbers and talked more and
more. Sometimes he'd call me from Spain, London,
or even Switzerland. I swear those guys are the
biggest thing in the world.

When the American Music Awards came around,
Sincere asked if I would be his date. But Mother
wasn't really feelin' that idea yet. So I asked, "Could
I have a date if *you* join us, Mother?"

"Me . . . join *you*?"

"I mean, can we *all* go together? Mother, you know
what I mean." I must've been out of my mind, 'cause
at any awards show it's always been Mother and I.

"I suppose we could do that. But we only have
two seats for the AMAs. The usual."

"Sincere already has tickets, Mother. I think each
member of NUBIAN has like two guests each."

"Really?" Mother thought about it some. "But are
they already inviting folks—that's the question. All
along, everyone knows that those boys always bring

their mothers to the shows. And the AMA people don't go for seat changing, it's TV, ya know."

I thought about that and it pissed me off how the awards shows only give some people one ticket, some two, and others more. There was a time when I wasn't even invited and if I was older, Mother wouldn't have been able to come. One ticket means one ticket. But because NUBIAN is like the biggest R&B group since the Jackson Five, they get the whole red carpet treatment. They even get a dressing room if they want. So Sincere and I sat in separate seats at the Shrine auditorium, looking across a hundred people just to see each other. They have a few breaks when folks can use the restrooms—but that was a joke, considering how everyone lined up like it's Off Track Betting or something. At least we got a chance to chat in the lobby during the break. The fans who are let in to see the AMAs are kept up top so that they don't crowd the celebrities with requests for autographs and photos. Still, a couple get through, and as I might've guessed, they nearly trampled me to get to Sincere. Someone even took a photo of us. Before you know it, my picture is all over the place as *"Sincere's new love interest," "Sincere's girlfriend."* ANGEL'S SINCERE one magazine read. Another claimed, ANGEL STARTS TO SOW WILD OATS!

*That one* kind of got me, tryin' to tell everyone how I'm a virgin who's lookin' to get her groove on. I felt better once I spoke with Sincere about the press. He told me that I should learn early how the press is usually no good and that they're always trying to stir up scandals. "You gotta expect that in this business," he told me. But, of course, Mother had already explained that to me. It was just that this was the first time it touched my personal life. I mean, I really liked Sincere. And now it was like my every move was being watched and highlighted. I even started to think my phone was bugged by *Right On!* or *Sister 2 Sister* magazines.

My brother was supposed to go with me to the People's Choice Awards, but he got sick. So I asked Mother if Sincere could go with me instead. She said yes! But I know what the answer would've been if she didn't have to stay home and take care of Tray. I spent many nights imagining what our date would be like. Wondering if he would be like Lefty—only *with* the moves.

Rory began to get jealous after all the press and stuff. He even started trippin', thinkin' I slept with Sincere and everything.

"You a video ho," he said. "You *deserve* a singer too, 'cause you can't kick it wit' a real G no more. We don't go for that celebrity shit." When Rory stepped off, I was like, *Ppppshhh! His loss!* And I did the two snaps and a circle *with* a neck twist.

He was lyin' anyway, 'cause that jackass was tryin' to get a record deal too. The whole thing made me think about Sincere even more, so much so that I would touch myself in bed at night. It felt so illegal, like I was violating the so-called virgin code. The one my mother made up.

# Chapter 5
## DOUGLASS

I know Rain was cursin' my ass out, callin' me all kinds of motherfucker this and motherfucker that, gritting and puckering like she had the tip of a sax pressed to her mouth. It's what she always did when she copped one of her infamous attitudes. Maybe I don't blame her since I was the one who convinced her to surrender; I was the one who convinced her that she needed me, and that her body, mind, and future belonged to me. After all, she left her secure, comfy, cozy home in Mt. Vernon for me. And while being an adopted child might not be the perfect circumstance, I knew she had zero responsibilities. All she had to do was play the role of sweet li'l Rain with the *yes, ma'am*s and the *no, sir*s. She could have kept that Li'l Red Riding Hood act going, and the world would have been hers for the taking. But that mask came off quickly after she became my companion. I mean, I had a few girlfriends before her, but *none of them* did the things that Rain did to me, including how she had me feelin' like her favorite meal as much as she licked and ate my body. And she *always* swallowed, like I was a year's supply of free cherry Kool-Aid. Rain was my ghetto fairy tale, the girl who couldn't say no. She had that

tight, petite body I liked to manhandle, and she had
a fair-skinned complexion that I loved to rub down.
And my dick got hard whenever I thought about
those dick-sucking lips of hers, lips that any man
would crawl for. I remember when Rain told me
about her ex-boyfriend turning abusive toward
her—abusing drugs and all. She said she swore off
men and didn't want anything else to do with them.
She even considered becoming a nun, turning les-
bian, or having the last laugh and die playing with
herself.

But of course I came along (Captain Save-a-ho)
with a good business head on my shoulders and, I
guess, I was all the "daddy" she wished for in life.
And she gave up all of those miserable thoughts of
suicide, making my life hers. She left her good-ass
job at the bank with less than a two-day notice and
she moved in to introduce me to the most incredible
sex I ever had—on demand.

**O**n the morning of our argument, I pulled into the
parking lot at the side of Marty & Lenny's. I
could see that there were a few performers who'd arrived early. The early ones were always the hungri-
est for success. They were standing on the sidewalk
outside of the club's wrought-iron gate, and a couple
of them rushed in my direction to help me gather
and carry various bags into the rehearsal. I could see
Chrissy, our stage manager, sitting in her white
Honda, and as soon as she spotted me, she jumped
out to spread all her joy and cheer. Somehow, I took
her diplomacies to be superficial. Yes, she was an inspired Broadway performer, and yes, she expressed

to me how she wanted me to teach her the business of TV and stage production. But the whole Pollyanna act was a bit much, as if her real-life appearances were part of an act.

And while I admit to being amused by her around-the-clock energy, her Dolly Parton breasts, her teased, platinum-blond hair, and that radiant smile, I couldn't help wanting to take advantage of all that endless energy. And on the other hand, the pessimist in me was waiting for Chrissy's flame to dwindle or get burning hot.

"Heeey, Deeee! Good morning! Where's Rain?"

I was suddenly reminded of how blessed I was to never have to wake up to *her* every morning.

"She's taking a cab over. Running late, I guess," I lied.

Chrissy didn't frown all the way before she asked, "Who's going to organize the schedule?" Chrissy's voice was good enough for radio, and far too superior for everyday conversation—crossing her *T*s with precision, clickin' and tickin' with a consonance worthy of some audience's applause.

"I'm taking care of that," I told her.

"Okay, D," she sang "but remember, the whole idea here is for you to stand back. You know, maintain a little authority. Think Roy Scheider in *All That Jazz*. You're the boss, so you've got to act the part. Play the role. Let us, the supporting cast, carry out your intentions."

I smiled inside, not wanting to get caught up in her hype or my ego. But I couldn't help it. Chrissy was infectious and I was enjoying it. Besides, Chrissy was right—as we'd discussed during the previous weeks—about bosses laying out the plan, the rules, and objectives. Directors see to it that the plan runs smoothly, while the supporting cast carries out the footwork until completion. Although I did conceive these ventures in entertainment (one after another), I couldn't help thinking that Chrissy—hungry, out-of-work actress that she was—was actually teaching *me* something.

"I gotcha, I gotcha. Let's just move along with this rehearsal as smoothly as we can. You and I can handle things if it comes down to that. . . ."

I was amused at how Chrissy ultimately bent over backward to satisfy our objectives (and my ego). Her charm teetered on the cliff of impressionable, and sometimes made me wonder if she was offering me her body. Maybe *that* was even her plan, the way she designed her relationships. For me, the flattery usually got somebody over. However, Chrissy always submitted to my raw power despite her undying sales pitches.

I told her, "Just look at these starving performers." I slipped the statement in before any of them got within earshot. "They just can't wait to jump when we say jump. So relax. We got this." I put my hand on her shoulder—a touch of confidence. Then with my pert smile, I closed the door of the Chevy. Chrissy adjusted the shoulder bag on herself and prepared to follow alongside me. That's when I got an idea.

"Jump," I told her out of the blue.

"Huh?" Chrissy uttered her giddy smile, not sure she heard me right.

"I *said* . . . jump. Right here, right now." I stood still, my head and expression buckling down to show

I meant what I'd said. She jumped. A bit perfunctory. More like a trite bounce. Her breasts barely jiggled. I leaned back against a car, unsatisfied. I wanted to see more emotion in that jump.

"That was a *bounce,* Chrissy. Now jump, like I *know* you know how. Jump!" I tried not to be too loud with others approaching us. She realized they were closing in and at this moment, her eyes excitedly desperate, she jumped, her breasts bouncing like water balloons.

"Now, what*ever* was *that* for?" Chrissy asked, adjusting the straps of her bra under that V-neck, sky blue top. Her question just hung there while she readjusted her shoulder bag. I moved closer to whisper in her ear and noticed for the first time that she stood a full head shorter than me with her buxom frame. I flaunted my self-proclaimed authority by putting my curled forefinger under her chin and saying, "Next time, don't question my moves. Otherwise you'll be questioning your own like you are right now. *Got it?*"

"Got it." Chrissy answered with slight shame. And from that moment on I knew she was like soft ice cream in my hot palm. A couple of the performers took some of the bags at our feet and we all made great strides toward the front of the club. It was five past ten as I led the way into the staring crowd. I also caught that little suggestion of scorn in Chrissy's eye, wondering if I was losing my mind or what. But she kept that humble mask on as we got busy with the auditions and settling the nerves of the twenty-plus performers in attendance.

"Good morning!" I broke the silence in the open air. The only other sounds were those of passing cars on nearby main streets and others entering the parking lot. Teenage boys and girls, some parents, and some in their twenties answered back cheerfully. I turned to face Chrissy (passing the baton, so to speak) and she took off with her blond ambition.

"*Okay*, people, I want to get a head count so that I can check you off on my list. As I call your name please step through the entrance . . ." Chrissy added that with a wee bit of emphasis, so that I would get the point to summon the manager of the club.

". . . and have a seat inside. If I'm not mistaken, the bar will be closed except for juice and soda . . . and all smiles, people. *Please*. Your best appearance begins now." Chrissy's face lit up as an example. "It's good practice for when the cameras start rolling. Remember, you're all going to be on *television*! So up with the attitudes, and deep, healthy breathing, okay?"

I was stuck somewhere between speaking with my manager on my cell phone and watching Chrissy in amazement as she filled the room and everyone in it with high hopes. In the meantime, I knew it was all hot air she was blowing.

"Okay, cool," I said into the phone. "'Cause we're outside and we need to get started." I shut the flip phone while my eyes virtually penetrated the building's exterior, willing the manager through the club, then through the glassy double-door entrance, and on up to the gates where he unlocked the padlock. As he removed the chain, Chrissy stalled with all kinds of spur-of-the-moment instructions for the growing crowd. There were more than thirty now, and I was suddenly damned proud of Chrissy for handling the group so well. She was another good choice I made since she, too, was once a performer in óne of our earlier talent showcases. She, too, used to be on the receiving end of instructions, waiting and nervous. So she knew "the walk" they were now walking. And now in her newly appointed position, she was coming so close to surpassing my expectations that I could actually say she impressed me—a difficult challenge. By now I'd had my fill of performers—meeting with them, coaching, and preparing them; so Chrissy was a good delegate for all these things I used to do—conveniently putting on her act as a stage manager.

The format for the *Westchester Talent Show* was such that every variety of performer imaginable would be accommodated. My idea was to promote it as a family event for young and old. The open invite provoked auditions by four-year-old crooners as well as eighty-four-year-old dancers. The concept drew an endless array of in-the-shower singers, dancers with formal training, models of every shape and size, poets, instrumentalists, and a variety of others, including magicians and jugglers. This show was a big enough opportunity for every living being in the region to have a reason to come and perform, even those who *didn't* think they had talent. Along with the variety of talent came a variety of cultures and nationalities; all with their various practices and idiosyncrasies. There were the hip-hop cliques, the heavy metal rock extremists, the subtle town folk, the organic farm boys and girls, the rural square dancers, and the makeshift dance troops that were groomed in the nearby housing projects. Some of the models were prissy, the rappers cocky, the rockers arrogant, and the folk singers scared as cattle in a meat-packing plant. All of that, plus a cross section of heavyweight gospel singers, necessitated my never-ending responsibilities as parent, friend, and sometimes executioner.

Chrissy counted the performers and had them sit on the dance floor at the center of the venue. I was already situated at a table in the rear. While the focus was on Chrissy, I could still feel everyone's eyes staring at me. Most of Marty's & Lenny's was dark. There were no skylights and no sense in wasting money on electricity when the club wasn't officially open for business. Stingy club manager. While I watched the rehearsal I answered my cell phone, knowing very well who was calling before I even looked at the caller ID. I listened to Rain's apology, but once she shut up I pummeled her.

"Yeah. Is *that* so? Well listen, I thought about your attitude and how you slammed the car door like you got no sense, and I think you should stay home." Coming from my lips, the words even *felt* like I was punishing her. After all, being the stage manager for the show and my personal assistant for all intents and purposes bestowed Rain with important responsibility. Responsibility that I was now heavy-handedly suspending. She'd grown to love my projects and the status it lent her.

I told her, "I don't need the negative vibes around me." I was expecting a vindictive response. And I got one.

"Well, I'm going to my parents' house, you ASS-HOLE!" The line went dead. I was shocked for a quick minute, but then I thought *Fuck it*, and it was business as usual. Rain would return. I was sure of it.

As I closed the cell phone, I recognized the girl who had auditioned about a month earlier. Janine was the bootylicious city girl with the fine curves and pretty Spanish eyes. More than ever, I realized why there was conflict that morning with Rain. I realized that I *wanted* an argument, an excuse to keep Rain away from what was about to go down. And at the time, I couldn't figure out whether it was fate or my dick that brought above these circumstances, but nonetheless the opportunity was here and now. I pressed my palms to my forehead and mashed it slowly down my grill as if to flatten the contours and features of my face. My left and right brain sparred for the truth, one side wanting to hide the fact that Rain was a big part of my life; the other arguing that Janine was one fly piece of ass just waiting to be claimed. In some ways, both voices were losing, outdone by the sparkle in Janine's eye. It erased all concept of right and wrong. Janine had caused this same hysteria weeks earlier, at her first audition; she had my whole supporting staff up in arms, wondering who she was and how she got here. A couple of the guys practically fell over themselves trying to get to know her, with their eyes popping out, admiring her perfection. Nobody could tell at first sight whether she was white or Hispanic, but regardless, they were as mesmerized as I was by her full lips and priceless features. She danced like a Vegas showgirl tinged with an equal balance of hip-hop energy. Even *Rain* was twisted by Janine's overall presence, and how some of her flame had suddenly been swept away, passed on to this newcomer. But Rain made it a point to introduce herself *and* her baby . . . injecting that "she thing" just in case, so that Janine would know that—come hell or high water—there was at least *one* staff member who was *not* up for grabs. But I was hip to that shit. I looked right past it too, knowing damned well that our son didn't guarantee wedded bliss, and it *definitely* didn't mean I was on lockdown.

Another thing: There was an unwritten rule among the people (mostly male friends) who worked for me during those two years of weekly talent shows: *There's to be no messing with the female performers.*

The other unwritten rule: *If there's gonna be any messing around, I get first licks.*

Shit, since I was the man who *made* the rules, I could bend or break 'em too. I'd broken them before with Kelly. She and I spent the weekend together with a Luther Vandross CD on repeat. She didn't win the $500 for modeling in the talent show, but I gave her a consolation prize for her performance in bed when I showed her how easily her knees could reach her ears. Kelly came to my place pigeon-toed on Friday, and she left bowlegged and dreamy-eyed on Sunday night. After Kelly came Yolanda. Woo-woo-*woooo!* The backseat encounter I had with her was one for the memoirs. While I was running up in her she cried out, *"Make me a star!"* Yolanda was one of those persistent performers, and she was just as persistent a woman, showing up unexpected at my front door, stepping out of a taxi in the middle of a snowstorm. She had on a long, black fur coat wrapping her snug as a bug in a rug. Since I rarely turned down a booty call, I invited her in. She didn't hesitate. Didn't say a word. She stepped into the foyer, and as I turned she opened her fur coat, dropped it to the floor, and posed butt-naked, hands up in the air like the fourth member of the Supremes. All the cool that I *thought* I had ran up out of my body as my jaw dropped and my eyes looked over this nineteen-year-old's God-given treasures. No sooner had I shut the door than Yolanda knelt down on her fur, loosened up my pants, and took me in her mouth like a hot-dog-eating champion.

So my experiences with women were pretty much salacious, selfish, and indulgent ones. It appeared as though most any woman could get caught in my net of entrepreneurial ventures. Most any woman, *including* Janine.

After Janine's first audition, and how she left me, Rain, and the rest of my staff in awe, there were a few other wayward phone calls between she and I. Nothing serious; just getting to know each other better. I learned that she was a Brooklyn girl, with a Brooklyn attitude and speech patterns that seemed rough against her God-given sensuality. And now that we were together at this latest gathering at Marty's & Lenny's, I felt it necessary to follow my heart . . . and my head.

# Chapter 6
## ANGEL

The People's Choice Awards was the usual, confused, celebrity-packed event that I've grown so accustomed to. Mother told me that whenever I meet someone, even if I've never seen their work, I should smile and act like I have. "Be diplomatic," she'd tell me.

"I love your work" was tattooed on the inside of my forehead, ready to be shared with anybody who even looked like a celeb. Even though Mother may have something there, in that it might engender a nice appreciation for me, I was not too happy with the idea. It's so cheesy and fake. I went to these shows and after-parties almost every week, and the praise seemed to run out of gas sometimes. And it got obvious, like I *obviously* didn't mean it. I mean, I might as well have opened up a phone book, made mad calls, and told everyone how marvelous their work is. So what if they hate their job cleaning up dog shit. Mother told me to say it.

Sincere was so cool. He even decided not to give out autographs for the night so that he could focus on me. I was flattered. Really. The limo took us to Roscoe's Chicken 'n' Waffles, and I felt more comfortable with more of our folks around. Even though

I was too formal in my sequined gown, people understood. Lots of rappers, singers, and actors filed into the place after us. I even saw Mike Tyson, Busta Rhymes, Eve, Redman, and Method Man. None of that mattered, 'cause Sincere was finally alone with me. We held hands in our booth, fed each other chicken wings, and toasted the future over some milkshakes. I felt so honored to have him all to myself when half the world would've bent over backward for his time. But here he was, interested in *me*.

"Hold my table," he suddenly told the waitress. Then he led me out through the back way to a passage that said EMPLOYEES ONLY. When we reached the back of the restaurant, nobody was there, and he spun me around and nudged me against the wall.

"I couldn't wait anymore, Angel," Sincere said right before he pressed up against me and gave me the sweetest kiss. I counted all ten seconds. I was feeling weak and in need of air, but I liked it. I put my arms around him—maybe so I wouldn't fall—and I kissed him back. Tongue and all. I immediately felt the pressure of having to show him I knew what to do. I mean, Rory and I have done a little kissing, but Sincere had been all over the world, probably with dozens of the most beautiful women begging him to kiss them. So I fed the frenzy and got as sloppy as I could until I really *did* need a chance to breathe. My eyes were still closed, and all I could think of was the birds in Minnie Ripperton's song "Loving You." My body was soft and my head was woozy. For the first time in a long time I didn't know what to do. I felt naked, like my clothes were still in the limo, my body was still in the fourth row at the PCAs, and my mind was one hour into the future. I was floating, drifting away on a stream of incredible feelings. He kissed me again, and my eyes stayed closed, revisiting that warm sensation—and then I was shook. A tremor rattled my bones the second Sincere felt me up. His hand was pulling my gown up over my hips until it grabbed my behind. Actually that wasn't the bad part. It was how he went behind and between my legs, slipped his fingers straight under my panties. That's when I lost it. I pushed him away from me. I mean, I didn't even know I was that strong to send him back up against the wall. That's when I ran back inside of Roscoe's and into the ladies' room. I didn't bother to fix my dress, I just felt it fall back into place. In the bathroom, I was a wreck. I was shivering like a freeze pop, my hands covering my face as I talked to myself.

"I can't believe he . . . I can't believe I . . . *Oh my . . .*"

I was beside myself. Humiliated and embarrassed. Afraid and alone. I didn't want to see him. My whole vision of him was distorted now and I couldn't imagine how it could ever be the same again.

"Angel . . ." Sincere was knocking on the bathroom door. My safe haven changed into a cage. He kept knocking. I just ignored it, though. I wanted him, the world, and myself to disappear. The knocking stopped, but not inside of my chest. I realized I was tense, squeezing my butt cheeks together like I was trying to stop something from gettin' up in there. Something like *him!*

"Hey, girl. One of them NUBIAN dudes is out there askin' about you."

*Oh no* . . . now I got the girl from *A Different World* all up in my face and my business. Lookin' at me like *Whatchu gonna do?*

Now, why did she suddenly look like a backstabbin' ho who wouldn't mind taking my place? Her hands on her hips and stuff. That got me goin'. I didn't know *what* I was gonna do or say, but I *did* know that I had to get out of *her* face.

"What? Baby . . . where you goin'?" Sincere's voice was just behind me, trying to keep up with me as I strutted out of the bathroom and through the restaurant with an agenda. I didn't care who saw me, or if I was keeping proper etiquette or not. I just wanted *out*.

"Take me home," I demanded when I got to the limo driver. He looked at me like I had just stabbed him, but he opened the door anyway. Sincere gave me space—I gotta give it to him for that, 'cause I don't know what I woulda done had he got in the limo with me. I waited as the limo driver and Sincere had a few words, then the car's engine started up. I took one of those so-so-deep breaths when the window lowered. Sincere peeked in.

I turned my head, cussing the driver under my breath.

"Sorry, babe. I told him to take you home." I let my lids flutter until they closed.

"Can I call you later?" Sincere, my dethroned Prince Charming, pleaded.

But my lips were sealed. Next thing I knew the limo was moving. And I didn't look back. I had mad questions when I got home.

*How long do I have to be a virgin? Everybody's doin' it but me. I know what goes where thanks to biology at Central High. So when can I get down . . . when can I get this monkey off my back? If I made the move, wouldn't today have been different? Was he makin' the right moves, and was I makin' the wrong ones?*

Funny thing about mirrors; they're just like dolls. They don't talk back. I swear I stayed in the bath for an hour and a half. Sincere called my private line so many times I had to adjust the answering machine to pick up on the first ring. Between his calls and Rory's before him—because I was steady erasing everything—the machine was working double-time. I was afraid it was gonna break and I wouldn't be able to retrieve my business calls.

I focused a lot more on my ever-growing singing career after the Roscoe's fiasco. We did a video for "Like That" and I became a popular image on B.E.T. and MTV. They played the song to death on the radio. My producer, Jingle, taught me a lot about the behind-the-scenes business, like the SoundScan numbers, the Billboard charts, and how I could make more money writing my own songs. I figured I'd better buckle down, since (it seemed) the world was putting me on this God-almighty pedestal. While I traveled on the major promo tour, taking trains and limos to stations from LA to Texas, Florida, and up the East Coast to New York, I began to write down my ideas for songs. Jingle gave me a formula to work with. He told me if there's a song I like by Whitney, Luther, or even Stevie Wonder, I should keep the melody in my head and just put my own words in place of the original lyrics. So I would hum "The Greatest Love of All," but I would write: "Whenever I'm Away." When I hummed the melody for "A House Is Not a Home," I would instead write: "Your Dreams Are Safe with Me."

I called Jingle while I was on the road, shared a few of my lines with him, and he assured me that I had good songs. I don't know if he was just pumpin' my head up or what, but I stayed excited. One thing Jingle told me, and which I never forgot was, "You're in a good place in the industry, Angel. Your music is being played on the R&B *and* pop formats. MTV, VH-1, *and* B.E.T. Not many performers can claim that type of crossover appeal. Just keep doin' what you're doin'," he told me.

The publicist from Artistic was Lianne. She was nice to put up with me for the whole tour, but I could see she thought I was wasting my time writing. Some of the radio personalities were real funny on the morning shows. My favorites were Doug Banks and Olivia Fox, Dr. Dre and Ed Lover, and Wendy Williams in New York. She keeps it ghetto. The local video shows were everything from cheesy to broadcast quality, but it seemed like there were public access shows galore. Like, anybody who wanted to start a video show could do it just by raising their hands. *Ooh . . . I'm a video producer!* And everybody's supposed to go *woo-woo-woo*, and bow down to them. I just kept Mother's words in mind. *Diplomacy, darling. Remember your diplomacy.*

I was excited when we reached New York. It was the end of the tour, plus I'd been to New York only once when the single was getting a buzz in certain markets. After the morning shows on WBLS, Hot 97, KTU, Power 105, and Z100, I had lunch with one of the label's vice presidents. It was a whole big deal at the Russian Tea Room, where we discussed my future and how I had to maintain a *certain image* to satisfy my fan base. I got the idea that he was caught up in all the hoopla about Sincere and I. Those damn fan magazines never stop with the gossip. The instant that I thought about Sincere again, I caught a chill below my stomach. It felt like a cramp, like my period was coming around again.

After lunch there were more video shows. Lianne scheduled interviews in half-hour segments, all to be done in the conference room at Artistic headquarters. Some of the hosts were weird, and I learned to appreciate them because they broke up the usual humdrum questions I got from the stupid hosts. I know I'm supposed to think diplomacy, but it's pretty hard when these folks are just plain ignorant. They sound like children sometimes, running the same old questions. You'd think that my fans already know how I got started and that they would get tired of hearing the same answer every time they turned the station or looked on my Web site.

# Chapter 7
## DOUGLASS

**S**aturday's big audition at Marty's & Lenny's turned into more of a play-it-by-ear atmosphere, instead of the well-planned rehearsal that we had laid out. Although I had a staff to help things move along smoothly, to keep things business as usual, performers were stalled by miscued cassette tapes or skips in the CDs, and others were too long with their stage shows, which had to be cut down. To top that off, Rain was trying every way possible to reach me, calling other staff members and the club manager and whatnot. But like I told everyone, I didn't care what she had to say. I turned off my cell phone and my pager, and I focused on more pleasant things.

Janine was something else to look at, perched up against a mirrored wall in the club, with her black spandex bodysuit so slick against her curves. She also had on a cute pair of white cross-trainer kicks, and a brown leather flight jacket that engulfed her upper body. With her hungry look, she could've been Madonna before Madonna became *the* Madonna. Or she could've been a mannequin, there to lure impulsive buyers. And a buyer I was! I couldn't help myself from stealing a look here and there at her perky breasts and her lengthy brunette hair tied back into a bouncing ponytail. Rain knew I liked the ponytail look, and she rocked her hair like that from time to time. So Janine seemed to fit right in with my likes.

At some point during the morning, I closed the gap between Janine and I with a convincing smile, and she reciprocated with her daring Spanish eyes. My ego roared, and my hormones stood at attention. I had to free myself of the fix she had on me, so I redirected my focus on the rehearsal.

Singers, rappers, dancers and comics took the stage one after the other, while Chrissy made notes and gave pointers to each performer.

*"Smile!"*

*"Face the cameras!"*

*"Take your time; you're making television history here!"*

*Jesus.* She really knew how to pour on the bull-shit. But she served her purpose, keeping things lively. Soon it was break time and the dim lighting made for a mellow atmosphere despite all of the energy and anticipation in the venue.

While chain-drinking ginger ale, I addressed some issues of music and lighting with the deejay. I then found an empty stool and sat down, just chillin' in a dark passage next to the sound booth. While all the other performers and staff members were toward the back of the club, or across the street at the mall having lunch, Janine showed up to ask me for a sip of my ginger ale. Was this girl direct or *what*! My mind began shuffling ideas around ideas, wondering if this was an indication that something was about to go down between us. I glued my eyes to her full lips

as they hugged the can, somehow finding more pleasure in the cold drink then I had.

"Can you cue this tape for me? I know it's supposed to be ready, but I was practicing all night . . ."

I still found myself guessing at Janine's nationality. But it hardly mattered with her so up close and
personal. As far as I was concerned, her nationality
was Pretty as Hell.

"Don't worry about it," I said. And I took the
tape, caught off guard by the electricity of our first
skin-to-skin touch. I didn't wanna start reading into
things, imagining something that might not necessarily exist between us, despite the sparkle Janine
had in her eyes. But if there was a sign on her forehead, it would say: ANYTHING . . . JUST ASK. So I'll
admit that I was confused—bewildered by my own
desire versus my need to keep a business attitude.
But at that point the male overcame the man in me. I
gave in to the heat and took a chance. Nobody was
watching. The deejay was busy rewinding her tape. I
took her hand gingerly and tugged her toward me.
With little effort on my part, Janine melted into my
arms. I lowered my head to hers and crossed tongues
with her. It was a warm kiss. And it could've been the
hot-'n'-cold contrast to the ginger ale, but I felt sensation enough to keep it long and thirst-quenching.
We parted for air and she backed up, showing surprise by what had come over her, covering her
mouth with a half palm. No gasp. No rebuking it.
Just silent appreciation in her eyes. Now I noticed
her eyes looked more Italian—rich with pride and
devotion.

"Wanna go for pizza after the rehearsal?" I asked.

Janine agreed and we kept a distance for the next two hours. By 4 p.m. Rain made that one last effort to call the club. The day's events were coming to a close.

"Aw, shit!" I exclaimed when I found out it was her calling. But it was too late. I had already accepted the call.

"Sorry, sir . . . she says it's an emergency," the bartender explained.

"Yes, Rain." I pouted. Frustrated.

"I'm at my mother's house," she claimed.

"Yeah . . . *and?*" I said, waiting for her to make a point.

"I . . . I just wanted to let you know where me and the baby were."

I could feel her struggling, and I made it even harder on her with my thick attitude. I had an agenda this afternoon, and she was *not* a part of it.

"Yeah . . . okay. Bye." I was abrupt and ready to put down the phone, hoping she'd read between *my* lines. Janine's body was calling me.

"Um . . . well . . . the exterminator may be coming over soon . . ."

"Yeah?" I said that, but I meant *So what!*

"The fumes aren't good for the baby, Douglass . . ."

*"And?"*

"And . . . we might have to come back to the house with the baby. We don't have anywhere else to go."

"I don't think that's a good idea. Your attitude was on some bullshit today. I don't need the problems right now." I said this, but what I meant was *I want the house to myself so I can do God-knows-what with Janine!*

"Where we gonna go?" she whined a cry I've grown so accustomed to. But I also knew she had rage (and a woman's sixth sense) bubbling under that sweet-talkin' voice of hers. I knew scorn was ready to surface any minute. I ignored her, looking over at Janine across the club as if she was a target for my bow and arrow. She was packed up, bag over her shoulder, and ready for anything (so it seemed) as she leaned against the club's exit door.

*Damn, you look sexy.*

It was time to leave. Time for pizza. Time for *whatever. Um ... um ... um ...* Sure there was (at least) the baby's health to consider, but I was nowhere *near* rational with this fresh slice of cream pie looking me right in the face.

"I'll get back to you," I told Rain. Then I hung up the phone. Taking Rain's call at the rehearsal was a big mistake, because it rushed my whole spicy experience with Janine in the car, at the pizza shop, and on the way to my house.

Now there was that one thought keeping me from enjoying myself completely with Janine: *I hope Rain don't show up to ruin my private party.*

Even though my pager and cell phone were off, Rain's messages still vibrated and beeped in my mind. And while all of *that* was going on, Janine was on her big adventure, following me into the house.

The first thing I noticed was my answering machine. The little red light was blinking more than an overdone Christmas tree. I ignored it, closing the door behind us and then setting the steaming pizza pie box down on the nearby coffee table. Janine's eyes wandered, surveying my living room–slash–office.

"May I?" Janine gestured toward the hallway leading to the rest of the house.

Reading her mind, I said, "Janine . . . I told you she's not here."

"I believe you . . . I *believe* you. I just wanted to check out your place."

I hit her with this *Yeah, right!* expression and nodded. In that moment it seemed like I had found her on-switch for aggression. She glided down my hallways and corridors like some vibrant, dancing investigator.

Over pizza, Janine and I were both honest about our respective relationships. She already knew about Rain. But *damn*, so did *everybody*.

But then I learned about the cop she was living with. And I asked plenty of questions, too. Not that her having a man lessened my erection any, because having Janine sitting so close to me, in my house, on my couch, was like living a fantasy—the so-called casting couch. *This is it!* I thought. *I'm sitting on it right here and now! And she's the one ready to audition!!!*

I could tell she wanted me, and I sho' 'nuff couldn't wait to get a piece of her. But I digressed some from the kissy-kissy move I had put on her earlier, because I could feel a tremor in my body. All of a sudden I was hesitant, and a bit overwhelmed at the same time, at how easy this all seemed. I acted busy, reaching for my phone, but she deflected my arm and moved her body in my direction. She lifted a leg over my lap, straddling me with her wrists draped around my neck; Janine attacked my lips and tongue with her fully opened mouth. But I was quickly soaked into thoughts of my position, her desires to be in entertainment, and the casting couch myth. I became a principle in the chemistry, the one who could grant the resources that she wanted, even if all it meant was extra exposure. So while Janine may have thought she was influencing my acceptance of her on a business level, I knew I was just satisfying my curiosity about being with a white girl—even if she was only part white and part Dominican. This was a first for me. She eventually stopped the kissing as I led her to my bedroom.

"Nice bed," she said.

"A li'l sumpin' sumpin'."

"Dag . . . and you got mirrors on the ceiling too?"

"Wait 'til you feel the mattress," I said, knowing that she ain't seen nothin' yet.

Next thing I knew, I was watching this woman in total disbelief as she undressed before me. She was so vibrant, as if she couldn't wait to show me something. There was nothing else to say. No hesitancy, no tremors . . . Shit, I was about to make all my homies proud! My heartbeat and lust were performing in a concert with my own passion. The excitement continued to build, turning up a notch with every new revelation. Janine's breasts—I swear—were a perfectly sculpted pair, standing up and sticking out. Nothing fabricated or exaggerated. These amazing body parts were enough to fill my hands and then some. Just damned incredible, *period*. The nipples on these beauties were something like the erasers on those thick, bulky pencils I once used in grade school. But they also called out to me, forcing me to act at once. My lustful tendencies directed me as I cupped her soft muscles until she pressed up closer against my clothed body.

I sat on the edge of the bed as she untied my Timbs, unharnessing my feet. Then I stood while she removed my shirt and pants. I turned on the stereo and then reached into my CD rack. My *The King and I* CD might have been an appropriate choice to describe the events taking place in my bedroom, but to set the mood, I pulled out George Duke's CD. I knew his song "No Rhyme, No Reason" would help to smooth the session along 'til completion. However, I wasn't thinking of how appropriate it was for the occasion:

> *Sometimes love*
> *has no rhyme and no reason*

Janine and I floated on my waterbed mattress, exploring each other like we'd never been here before; Janine was hunting for the beast, while I was fishing for fresh salmon. She kissed me from head to toe. At one point she looked up at me with the most pensive expression; then without an answer from me, she took me in her mouth. I hate to act like all blow jobs are the best in the world—*they aren't*. But not this girl's! She treated my dick like sucking it was her job as well as her pleasure. It was wet and noisy and . . . and . . . *Damn,* I wanted to give her every penny in my bank account! Her mouth stayed active for quite some time, and it took every ounce of discipline I had for me not to shoot my spunk off before it was time.

Then she let up and continued kissing my upper body, my ears, and my neck. I couldn't take it much longer—my ejaculation was suspended only by my awe. So I reached into a drawer on my nightstand for a rubber and handed it to her. Propped up on her bended knees, she rolled it onto me, and then hovered over my chest while reaching between her legs. She grabbed me firmly, like a fist controlling a joystick of a video game, and guided me in, inviting me into her moist folds. Janine wiggled her pelvis, lowering herself more and more, squeezing me snugly inside of her. I couldn't hide my excited eyes—not that she was paying any attention to them as she raised her naked and free arms over her shoulders, clutching her ponytail on top of her head. Her eyes were looking through partially closed lids at the mirrors above us when she finally landed against my hips, those wanton lips between her legs clenching me fully inside of her. She was wet, soaking me underneath her. She was breathing loud, like my new central air conditioner, with her carnal exhales escalating along with the friction. My own breathing seemed constricted. I wanted to let go, but letting go seemed so final. And I wanted this to last. Janine continued to moan. Her motions on top of me became more and more lively. We rolled with the current of the water-filled mattress under us, and at other times, against it.

At some point, she began bouncing, slapping her hands on my bare chest, while bucking on top of me. A frenzied, dancing ponytail was all I saw at

times, until Janine gave up that exhausted gasp—
that uncontrollable release—and she slumped over,
her breasts against my chest. Still moaning and digging her body into mine, her face was now cradled
in my armpit as I reached for dear life. My insides
were screaming for some release. Janine slowed
down and asked, "You want me from behind?"

*Do I?*

Her eyes were deep, seeking the depths of my
own. A bead of perspiration trickled down her tem-
ple. My answer went unspoken as we shifted, balanc-
ing on the waves below us. Behind her now, I
suddenly realized what beauty was all about. Shallow
as I cared to be, beauty was this beautiful woman's
fine, round ass, extended and bare before me for the
taking. Anticipating my entry, bent over on all fours,
Janine looked back—half excited, half frightened.
Back to where I was most comfortable, I slipped inside of what looked like a living, breathing peach, but
what felt like some slimy hand cleaner within a
warm, throbbing grip. I rested there on my knees,
hands gripping her sides, basking in her glory. Deep
as I could be in it. Janine eventually dropped down,
flush against the sheets, and her hands clenched the
abundance of pillows over her head. She was coming
again.

Her waist and ass arched in an upward slope, connecting with me, the driver. Friction. Water sounds.
Music. Animal moans. Each sensation outdid the one
before, our bodies becoming a blend of giving and
taking, pushing and pulling. Janine writhed and
squealed, pleasing my ego tremendously. Her ass and
my groin were new best friends. The emotion built

up to exhilaration and ecstasy, and I wasn't gonna wait anymore. I *couldn't*. Our rhythm eventually contradicted the smooth music, and we got loud and obnoxious with it. I pressed her face into the pillows nose-first, muffling her cries. Her ass continued to feed me back as much as I was bumping and smacking it. I could see her hands grip the pillows one last time before I busted off inside of her—a water hose of lust. I collapsed on top of her back like a seal, molding to her contours with my weight.

**S**atisfied, we laid there for what seemed like forever. Floating. In the meantime, the red indicator lights were blinking on my phone. One line after another. For all the wrong reasons, I was so glad for the silent-ringer option on my phone system. Still, it was time to act on my common sense. I urged Janine to get up. It was getting late. We got dressed, pulling clothes over our own fumes of sex, and quickly cleaned up. She knew as well as I did that my home was also home to another woman. Another woman who might show up at any moment. So we hurriedly said our good-byes. I rushed her to the train station and after a luscious kiss, we promised each other that we'd do it again. Very soon.

**I**t is said that there can be no pleasure without pain. But, just like anybody else, I never expected the pain. Never saw it coming.

I kept my distance from Rain when she came back to the house. The distance would've lasted much longer if not for our child. Besides, she was so damn convenient around the house—for managing the business I ran, for doing the housekeeping, for shopping for food, and for sex. Before she returned, of course, I removed all evidence of my Dominican-Italian rendezvous. The pizza box. The drinking cups. The wrapper for the condom. And I didn't forget to change the sheets on the bed or to check for hair in the bathroom sink. I covered all of my bases like I had committed the perfect murder.

Saturday turned to Sunday, and I was busy with one of the performers—a singer who came all the way from Connecticut to have me remove the vocal tracks from a song she would use for the upcoming show. I did this for a small service charge so that performers could use almost any song as an "instrumental only" track to perform to. So, with her boyfriend by her side, the singer and I sat and conversed in a quiet, professional manner while my electronic gadget played the instrumental results over the home audio system. At once, I turned to see Rain sitting at my desk, organizing things as she normally would, and being nosy with my bills and notes and such while arranging them in neat piles. A fit of desperation overcame me, knowing what Rain might now find in front of her. And in that brief moment I put my hand to my face, realizing what I had done.

Murphy's Law did *not* fail. Rain's expression turned to outrage as she reviewed my handwriting. Then she turned to me. I could've swallowed a frog as paranoia raced through my body. Rain shot up and out of my executive chair, mumbling, "*A five, huh? I'll* give you a FIVE!" she ranted, and stormed out of our presence as my two visitors sat stunned. I excused her actions in her absence as if I didn't know what she was talking about. But Rain was back in less than a blink of an eye.

"I can't *believe* you! After everything I've *done* for you! You had to go and FUCK THAT BITCH!" Rain was on fire, speaking directly to the three of us. My houseguests had their jaws locked open. Rain stomped back into the house, yelling now, while crashing and banging commenced in the back, out of our eyesight.

I hurried the two out of the office. They assured me that no explanation was needed, but I think that Rain scared the shit out of them and that they didn't want to sink with my ship. Behind closed doors, I wagged my head, cursing my own stupidity. My mind raced back to the idle notes I made at my desk—notes regarding the various women I'd fucked and what they were good at, rating them on a scale of one to ten. Naturally, Rain knew of my past involvements, so seeing a few *new* additions could only mean one thing: that I was cheating on her. And to make matters worse, since Janine's name was the last name on that list, Rain could rest her case; she had enough evidence to know I'd been a busy boy sometime within the last two weeks. Not to mention I gave Janine an eight rating, while Rain got only a five. It was enough for Rain to bug out on me. We argued. We fought. And the relationship we had for more than two years was over. She moved out— back to her adoptive family. There were a few booty calls after that, but the relationship was dead. Rain and my son disappeared and I never saw them again. I missed Rain for, maybe, a day before I filled her shoes. And (thank God) her replacement was as freaky as she was, because the sex that Rain had provided was addictive enough to leave a brother strung out. It was in the aftermath of our big breakup that I vowed to stay single and unattached. Instead, I focused on building the TV show and interviewing more and more celebrities to build my credibility and track record for professional work. Small names led to big names, and every name garnered another endorsement.

No matter what my sexual misadventures amounted to, there was no denying that I was good at what I did outside of the bedroom and I could easily handle relationships with women who passed through my world.

# Chapter 8
## ANGEL

**H**ere we go again. I never met this group, but at the rate I was going, doing public access shows almost everyday, there seemed to always be new faces. Nothing special. Lianne prepped me for this "superstar" group. She said they had a show that was sharp, growing, and that it reached over two million viewers a week. So I had to stay on my toes; *some* of those viewers must be fans of mine. Even if only a few hundred of them listened to my music, I was ready to show 'em my best side.

"Of course we met before—when your first single got a buzz. You were only in New York for a hot minute, but Lianne called me right over to meet you. Lemme find out you don't remember me."

He was, like, a whole foot taller than me, and introduced himself as Doug, the producer of the show. But even *that* wasn't a big deal, because it seemed like every Tom, Dick, and Harry hosted a show, lugged around cheesy equipment, and called themselves "a producer." The bottom line, I guessed, was that they had only a little money and had no choice but to do everything on their own. I can't hate. And, well . . . at least this superstar guy had two assistants. All of 'em were cute and professional, too. This, I appreciated.

"Okay, right. *Now* I remember. You gave me that hockey jersey," I said before he kissed my cheek.

"Now you're talkin', Angel. You had me worried there for a minute. . . ."

"It's just . . . I meet so many people."

"Well, here's a few more for you to meet. This is Darryl, my cameraman, and this is Rick. He'll be snapping photos for our magazine."

"You got a magazine, too?" These folks were looking more and more legit.

"Mmm-hmm . . . ta-da!" the guy crooned, and presented me with a copy of *SuperStar Magazine*. I was on the cover with my braids wrapped like an African queen and my "number two" smile. Number two was the modest one.

"Wow. This is sharp." I began flipping through it.

"It's a mix of celebrity exclusives and community development. We call it a *cultural experience*."

"I see. . . ."

"And it's free, too."

"You're kidding. You've got to be joking. Something this good? Free? *Why?*"

"Yeah . . . the two-dollar price on top is just there to give the publication importance, so when people pick it up or if we hand it to 'em, they feel as though we're giving them something substantial . . . something of value. You'd be surprised at how gifts trigger a sense of obligation."

"*Wow* . . . I've gotta show my mother this—ya know we give out grants and stuff. Sometimes even as much as twenty-five to fifty grand." As I said this, I was steady checkin' my centerfold spread in the magazine. They must've gotten the photos from Lianne, I guessed.

"That sounds interesting. Keep us in mind."

"Oh definitely."

"So . . . I heard you already ate. Are you nice and comfortable? Ready for this interview?"

"Sure."

It looked like the camera was already rolling. And the guy he called Rick was already snapping photos. Doug was seated next to me, close enough for our legs to brush one another now and again. Doug didn't have a cheesy setup like I'd seen on too many occasions—the make-a-wish crews with a little RadioShack mic on a wire, attached to a home video camera. Naw, I could see that these guys were on their A-game. They had a studio camera and a couple of wireless lavaliere mics. Doug attached one to my shirt collar and his; then we did a brief sound check.

"We've been checkin' you out, ya know. You ain't no slouch, girl. Commercials. A TV sitcom. The appearances on Disney and Nickelodeon. Now you're hitting us with a whole album. Is it ever gonna stop?"

When hit with hard, direct praise, I couldn't help but blush. He had this way of forcing me to talk about everything. It was a different approach he took, to lay it all out before me instead of asking me the usual okey-doke questions. That would've been a step back after impressing me so. Doug made it so I *wanted* to talk. He was spinning images of myself at me with all of the various endeavors I'd taken on. This guy really did his homework!

"Thank you. It does seem like a lot, the way you

put it. But honestly? I love this business. I love to entertain, to do my thing. I don't really pay attention to how many appearances I've made here or there, I just go with the flow. It's like I'm part of this hurricane and it hasn't stopped yet."

"And now, you've taken a serious step by droppin' a hot album and the video for 'Like That.' It's got that whole *SuperStar* flavor, and we *love it,* Angel. I've also noticed a pattern in your work. In *Mama's House* your character's name is Angelique. For this project you've come out as Angel, and it all grows from your given name, Angelica. Was this all planned?"

I smiled at the accounting of my name and said, "No . . ."

"Is it a progression?"

"Yeah. I'm progressing . . . growing up. Everything's moving so fast. I'll be sixteen next week."

Doug was so relaxed, sitting next to me on the couch as if we were in someone's living room. Just chillin'. Then he did this thing—he looked into my eyes all sincere and slowly viewed my body up and down to where my pants gave way to my naked calves. I felt a chill and then I blushed again.

# Chapter 9
## DOUGLASS

**A**ngel was indeed "Like That," just like her song said. Her breasts were sittin' all up in my face, so Texas-sized for a sixteen-year-old, with skin like lightened coffee. She didn't even *look* fifteen or sixteen. She looked twenty-five with her little ankle bracelet, strap-up sandals, and a canary-yellow blouse with the neckline just below the collarbone. She had on black pants that matched her braids, like they were dyed in the same pot of ink. Coordinated. I was absorbed in her high cheekbones. Her clever, sparkling pupils were so inviting and her braids laying against her head and face, falling about her bare neck, looked like licorice dipped in molten caramel. This wasn't the cutie-pie from the sitcom, or the teenager I had met months earlier. This was a blossoming woman. Only getting better with time. I tried to look past the vocal prodigy and precious charmer that Lianne tried to push on me. But I didn't have to try hard. Angel was filling me with her depth of character, flashing those brilliant eyes while telling me, "Music is in me; I sing about the truth and what I believe in."

**I** can't lie—although I had interviewed the best singers, and even some of the world's most popular actresses, I was falling hard for Angel. Something about her was down to earth, telling me to lay this music and celebrity stuff to the side, because the most important thing here is me. What *I'm* about and what I've come to give to the world. The whole spell she cast had me open. I wasn't about business anymore. So what if I was twenty-eight years old, almost thirteen years older than her? Who was looking? Angel was alone with us in the conference room at Artistic's offices. Lianne checked in on us once—peeked in the door quickly and closed it just as soon. Darryl was roaming with the camera, MTV-style. Rick was sitting close by, probably just as caught up as I was.

"So what's your free time like? I read in some magazine that you were with somebody." I was meddling for sure, but we'd grown so comfortable in our short time together that I felt licensed to ask what I wanted. Angel's eyes turned from dreamy to unnerved.

"I heard about that. It was nothin', really. We did a single together on my album. That's all." It was obvious that she didn't feel like elaborating. And sure enough, she changed the subject. "I *did* have a boyfriend who grew up near me in San Diego. But he got beside himself."

"Yeah? Whaddaya think, he was jealous of your fame? Did you make him comfortable and explain things to him?"

"I did. I really *did* try. Even introduced him to my producer, to work on his own demo . . ."

"Did you explain to him about the press and how they make things up?"

"Yup. We went over all of that. He *still* flipped on me. Said I wasn't gonna be nothin' without him. That's when he had to go." Angel made that gesture with her arms and pointed fingers, like a traffic cop saying *You go that way.*

"So you're ridin' solo now?"

"Basically." Angel's shoulders slouched, shrugged humbly, as if she had been left no choice.

"Are you just saying that to sell more records? 'Cause I know how the labels do their artists."

"No. I'm *really* single. Hardly have time for socializing."

I believed her.

Rick and Darryl had to be kicking themselves in the background, seeing how Angel was so open with me. The touching and now the handholding.

"So humor me. It's five years into the future. You've got three to five platinum and double-platinum albums. One flopped and one was modest in sales. You've had thirty magazine covers, including *Vogue, Ebony, Essence, Cosmo, VIBE,* and of course *SuperStar.* You're smokin' hot. So tell me what's next on your agenda at age twenty?"

"Wow . . . that's a mouthful! Lemme think. I know I want my own place . . ."

"Yeah . . . you definitely wanna drop that momma's-girl image you got."

"Oh no! You didn't go there!" Angel laughed hysterically with me. We both knew it to be true. The fan magazines couldn't be getting *everything* wrong. The laughing died down with Angel wiping away merry tears.

Then she said, "But seriously, I do want to be on my own. *With* a car, thank you. A Jaguar would be just right with me."

"Okay, now that we've gotten past the shelter and material items, is Angel with a man? Possibly married? Are there some other entertainment ventures?"

"A man? I can't say. I'm fortunate that my family is still a unit. I *have* a father, a good father figure to direct me. So I won't necessarily be lookin' to fill a . . . a . . ."

"A void?"

"Right. No voids here. A man can't do nothin' for me that I can't do for myself."

When she said that, I was thinkin', *Oh brother*. This must be some women's lib shit. And maybe that was just "the Captain" thinking like the opportunist he was. But she continued.

"As far as entertainment goes, I wouldn't mind another sitcom, hopefully my own. I've been hoping for a movie, so maybe by then I'll have a couple of movies under my belt. And of *course*, I'll still be doing music. I've been writing songs for a little while now . . ."

"So you're a poet now?"

"I guess. Songwriters *are* poets."

"Okay, so drop us a jewel, Miss Angel."

Angel thought for a moment, then lit up as if she had an idea.

*"There's something I need to know.*
*I need an answer, tell me for sure.*
*I hate this pain that floats in the air,*
*so please help me.*

*Please save the lame explanations.*
*Don't even beat around the bush.*
*This thing we had, has it changed?*
*Is it true? Are we closing the book?"*

"Wow, Angel, that's some deep stuff. You sure you wrote that?"

"Mmm, about eighteen hours ago. It's fresh out of the frying pan."

"Hot. *Hot!* I can see it. You're sensational. Okay, before we go, I brought you a little gift."

"Did you?" Angel said, perched on the edge of her seat. That big smile could've been a chain of diamonds.

"Close your eyes, otherwise it won't be a surprise."

She did. Then I readied my best singing voice.

*"May tomorrow be a perfect day.*
*May you find love and laughter along the way.*
*May God keep you in his tender care*
*'Til he brings us together again."*

"Ohmigosh, you didn't . . ."
"I did."
"You wrote that?"

"I didn't. That's a little ditty that Donnie and Marie used to sing at the end of the TV show they used to have."

"Who are Donnie and Marie?" she asked seriously.

I got a laugh out of that, suddenly realizing that Angel and I were nearly a generation apart and that my head was too busy with TV nostalgia.

"They were once popular singers on TV. Not like the legends Whitney Houston or Diana Ross or James Brown are. But their music will last forever. And speaking of forever, I hope you enjoyed my li'l gift and that you, too, will last forever." I did the sign-off bit for television. Angel and I did some more publicity photos, and I asked Darryl and Rick to leave us for a moment.

Once Angel and I were alone and standing before each other (she with her thumbs in her back pockets, me with the folded arms), I got personal.

"You know, set all the entertainment aside, you're some piece of work . . ." She blushed and looked at the floor. I took her chin with my curled forefinger.

"Any chance a small-time, New York entrepreneur can get with a pretty-ass girl like you?"

Angel's eyes lit up, and she said, "Comin' on kinda strong, ain'tcha, Mr. *SuperStar*?"

"Please, call me Doug. *Dougie* if you'll let me be your pet."

Angel chuckled. I moved in. Kissed her sweetly on the cheek. "No need to answer that now, angel eyes. Just know that whatever you do, wherever you go, I'm interested."

Angel and I exchanged phone numbers.

# Chapter 10
## ANGEL

I'm feelin' Doug. He was too cool as a television host, and too smooth as a man. Sweet enough to eat. I wanted to call him the minute I got back to LA, like I was missing something. Of course there's the whole thing about pursuit and how (Mother says) a guy should call on a girl first. But that was then. Today's *Cosmo* woman is taking things into her own hands and I definitely wanted him in *my* own hands. I waited anyway. My label budgeted a second video for me. It was set to be shot in Times Square in New York. I smiled when I heard that I'd be returning there, possibly for a four-week stay. I hoped Doug would call so I could meet him. Mother has been letting me go off on business trips alone lately. She trusts Lianne. But if she knew Lianne like I know Lianne (the party animal), Mother would be riding shotgun, by my side. The Soul Train Awards came around and I was asked to be a presenter. I would've been nominated for Best New Artist, but my album wasn't released in time to be considered. All I can hope is that my album will stay strong through the year so that they'll remember me next time around. So far my "Like That" single is number two on Billboard's R&B chart and top 10 on the pop charts. I noticed that the better my songs do on the charts, the more opportunities come around. I've also been checkin' other female artists who have projects out. Janet is on the charts too. The last single of her most recent album was already number one on all the charts and had been there for, like, thirty weeks.

I'm supposed to be happy she doesn't have anything in the top ten now because, Lianne says, it would be a lot harder for me to reach the top slot. It's crazy . . . I mean, I just wanted to sing, to make folks happy with my music. And all of a sudden I'm in this competition. All kinds of competitions: the Grammies, the AMAs, the Soul Train Awards, the moon man at MTV, and on and on and on. It doesn't seem to stop. Jingle tells me to ignore all of that—the charts, the awards and the competition. He said to just do what I love and follow my heart. Mother said that was sage advice. I was happy to hear that too, 'cause I love Janet's music, and Madonna, Whitney, and Beyoncé and the others too. Now, because I'm pushing a product, I'm supposed to hate? *Pppppshhh! Puulease.* I hope I never have to go up against Whitney. That's my girl.

I got nervous at the Soul Train Awards. I'm not sure if it was because NUBIAN was performing or because it was my first ever presentation on the show. I had to beg Mother to work it out so there could be four tickets for the show. 'Cause they got all fussy last year and gave us only two. This year I was a presenter, plus they wanted me to sing "Like That." Sincere and me in the same show . . . of all the luck. Mother told me it was no problem this year with tickets.

"You're *big* now, girl. They're throwin' you tickets. Throwin' them."

So Tray came, my father and mother, and Lianne sat with us. It made me comfortable on stage. Rehearsal was the day before and I avoided Sincere like the plague. I just didn't feel like drama. And seeing his face just reminds me of his hand all on my stuff that night behind Roscoe's.

I was filled with the spirit; singing in front of so many celebrity folks. It's crazy, 'cause I've done Disney and Nickelodeon where, like, there were twenty or thirty thousand people in the audience. Probably millions on TV, but I can't *see* them. At the Soul Train show everybody who was anybody was there. I felt like I was under Janet or Beyoncé's microscope, Whitney's magnifying glass, and behind Diana Ross's mirror. They were giving Diana Ross the Lifetime Achievement Award, so she was in the front row. I started singing the chills off. Nothing incredible, just like, introducing folks to my voice. I wore this sequined gown that Mother rented from Dolce & Gabbana. She says that we've gotta rent those types of dresses because they go out of style too fast, but I think she was just looking out for my finances. By the second verse, I began to loosen up. I was warm now, and doing what I learned in acting class—projecting myself so that, if possible, every single person in the Shrine Auditorium would think I was singing to them exclusively. I started doing acrobatics with my voice, stretching my notes and lacing certain lyrics with vibrato. When I hit the bridge I went to church, and the audience went wild. I saw Diana Ross smile. She smiled! Now I was sure I was doing the right thing. The applause gave me more energy and I finished the song like a bird still in flight. I bowed and the director yelled cut. Lianne waited by stage left. She gave me a hug, and over her shoulder I saw him. Couldn't help it. He was standing right there. Sincere made a silent clapping gesture and I showed the slightest appreciation with a nod. Then Lianne led me to the dressing room. Flowers were waiting for me. Douglass. I took that to be his first call, and it justified my call to him.

"How did you do that?" I asked him the next day on my private line. I was relaxed in my Honey Dip T-shirt and panties. He didn't know what I was wearing, but I felt naughty with him in my ear and being half-naked.

"Let's just say I know a few people. Sorry I couldn't be there; I'd have given them to you personally," he told me. I thought on that, thrilled at the idea of my new friend in the face of that fresh boy Sincere.

"They were *so* sweet, Dougie . . ."

"Now see, you can't call me that. Yet. Remember? Only if I can be your pet."

"Well, can you just be my pet for the moment? Don't go messin' up my groove."

"I guess. You comin' to New York soon?"

"They're shootin' 'Break It Down' in three weeks. I might be through there for a whole month."

"With Moms?"

"No! Well, I'm sure she'll be there for some of it, but she's goin' back to LA. She can't be with me the whole time."

"Know where you're staying?"

"The label usually puts me up at the Marriott, but this is supposed to be a special stay; they're pampering me. So I might be staying at the Waldorf-Astoria."

"Okay, big-time," he kidded. Then said, "I'll be holdin' my breath."

"Me too. Thanks for the flowers." When I hung up the phone I caught myself playing with my nipple. It felt good. Thinking of him somehow felt better.

# Chapter 11
## DOUGLASS

**A**ll the while I was holding my hard dick in my hand. Stiff as a 2 x4. It just couldn't be *this* easy. Angel was making innuendos that left so much to the imagination. I had her poster up on my wall now—over the bed. So every morning and every night she was the first and last person I saw. When I hung up the phone, I decided to go for it. I was fully clothed and lying on the bed with my feet hanging off the side, looking at myself in the ceiling mirror. This was indeed a strange sight. Doing myself. Watching the activity, then looking at the poster. I thought about her doing the things that Rain would do. I pictured her head bobbing up and down while I watched her on top of me, bouncing like a baboon, or her licking my ass. That last thought made me spit semen all over my clothes. But I didn't give a fuck at this point. It felt damn good to be relieved. I laid there, immersed in afterthoughts. Coming back to my senses, eventually coming to terms with reality and the far-fetched possibilities.

*Angel and me? Her freakin' me? Not in this lifetime,* I figured.

At the least I'd have to teach her. The erection

started again. I got up to shower before this got out
of hand.

After my father blew the lease-option agreement
that I orchestrated a few years earlier, the owner
made arrangements to come back and take posses-
sion of the house. There were some *damned good*
times in that house. The one-night stands that big
house was responsible for; the mini-orgies and the
barbeques we threw just to have girls stopping by.
Seems like the more rooms your crib has, the easier
the panties dropped to the floor. And it all made me
wonder if the magic was me or that damned real es-
tate. Still, it was an incredible ride that came to a
sudden halt.

But, regardless of where I lived, I had enough
cash flow from the magazine's ads and the side promotions I was managing—thanks to being seen in
two million homes each week—that I could afford
to move to a $5,000-a-month loft in the industrial
district of New Rochelle. *SuperStar*'s growth was
amazing. I added a modeling element to my ventures called The Black Model, which enabled me to
further monopolize the treasure chest of females
who aspired to be a part of the entertainment industry. I never thought of how dangerous this field was
for a man—*especially me*—to get into. As wayward
as I was with my dick, and being the womanizer that
I was? It was an experience that was begging for a
crash landing. Nevertheless, I followed my instincts.
And with little advertising, a river flow of bodies
migrated to the *SuperStar* offices—traffic that left
other tenants miffed. I had the loft set up to dazzle a

newcomer's mind, with photos, posters, videos and music to capture it all. The sea of full lips and baby-makin' hips that came knockin' at our door frightened the landlord and the other tenants who were all white, involved in common crafts like pottery or wicker-basket making, and always suspicious of how I made money. The activities I indulged in at the loft varied from day to day—I was hard to peg or pigeonhole. So the curiosity simply continued.

Express deliveries were a mainstay each and every day, bringing FedEx, UPS, and the USPS minutemen to our office at any given time. It gave me the substance and credibility that helped to stifle suspicion. After all, why would anyone send express packages to this guy, with his little loft space, almost every single day, unless he was important? His business must be of great concern to somebody, somewhere. So he must be legit. How easily average people were fooled.

I know the wonder and amazement was thick around me. I also know that the jealousy and envy interfered with *someone's* sleep.

**M**eanwhile, my editing and production skills had come a long way over the years. This was our fifth season on television, longer than Arsenio's run. Record labels began to send more than just videos to our offices. Now limousines were pulling up with established artists who needed to reach the *Super-Star* audience. On some occasions they'd stop by just to schmooze. Depending on the artist, we'd go out to eat at the local diner, or after a concert we'd visit a strip club around the way. All the while, local colleges were sending us interns, who applied to contribute their free labor to our growth, while they got to learn the business and develop behind-the-scenes experience. I screened these students for a specific female-only atmosphere that I wanted to maintain. They were either real pretty with no savvy and had to be taught, or they were so-so and had so much energy that I could count on their hard work and devotion to duty. Either way, I had more than twenty girls; seventeen-and eighteen-year-olds gliding in and out of my little world, providing plenty of inspiration with their pubescent presence. They were all hungry, and collectively, they motivated me with plenty of reason to get up early in the morning, even when I didn't want to, and plenty to look at when I did.

While I kept college interns busy with menial tasks such as reviewing and logging incoming videos, keeping records and inventory of our video library, and sifting through the mail for new story ideas for the magazine, it was still necessary to pay a girl to cover the tasks that I might delegate.

Since the cable show shifted directions and became an all-black format, Chrissy lost interest. Her thing was Broadway and live performance, not black entertainment. The live amateur performances died out since we changed our focus to television production and established acts who were looking for exposure in the various markets where *SuperStar* aired. Not only that, the record labels that supported and promoted these very artists purchased advertising in our magazine in a kind of you-scratch-our-back-and-we'll-scratch-yours kind of way. The labels also sent us big-name acts as well as new ones, and we either interviewed them or incorporated them into some live performance sponsored by local businesses that advertised with us. Darryl was still the man to call on for video shoots, and Rick was available to host any live shows and promotions that we sponsored. But both of them kept day jobs apart from their interest in *SuperStar*. So ultimately, I was the head cook and bottle washer when it came to the leg work behind the company. That is, until Deidra came along.

I stumbled upon Deidra at another label within Manhattan's Time Warner building. There must've been twenty record labels under one roof, occupying every bit of the twenty floors. And since I dealt with the video, publicity, and promotion departments for each label, I literally had dozens of people to see and to push up on when I needed certain things. It afforded me a freewheeling presence, to come and go and impose where and when I needed to. I never left the Time Warner building without a few hundred dollars' worth of CDs, tapes, or concert tickets since I was doing so many favors for so many departments under the same umbrella. The singles—with one or two songs on them—were given to my interns. The full-length CDs, from the most obscure artists to the latest top-selling albums, helped to build a library of thousands of titles to feed my insatiable appetite for music. Concert tickets came to me so frequently I had to send others to fill my seat. And if I was short on dough, I'd just sell them.

During one of my record company tours, I ran

into a new face—a new personality—who so impressed me with her energy and tact that I went beyond the usual routine. Deidra juggled phone calls, kept notes, and managed my requests so meticulously, so effectively, and with such a pleasing smile to go with her actions, that I acted on impulse. I strutted back down to the street level to buy a bouquet of fresh flowers, and left them for her when she was away from her desk. When I returned to the loft, Deidra's message was on my machine. She was clearly choked up about the flowers. When I returned the call, the emotions poured out in real time. She sobbed and carried on about how nobody ever did that for her, not even her boss appreciated her work, and so on and so forth. Her response truly caught me off guard as well, because I hadn't calculated my actions. They were the result of some uncontrollable reflex. I honestly didn't have an ulterior motive in mind.

And yet, Deidra quit her job a few days later and showed up at my office with pools of ambition in her eyes. During our sit-down discussion I learned a few things.

"Why are you so nervous?" I asked her after we got past the initial small talk. "I'm an entrepreneur, not a therapist," I told her.

"Well, all I've been through, I probably need a surgeon too; someone to transplant my heart and mind. To help me get rid of this luggage I've got."

Deidra was a honey-dipped cutie, with more ass than breasts, but a pretty face to balance out what some might note as her inequities. Plus she was

wearing a ponytail—and that was a *big* plus, if only
because it satiated my fetish.

"See, I've just left my job at the label."

"*Really*. But you seemed so important to them.
Part of the woodwork."

"Believe me, I was. My boss is *still* calling me,
begging me to come back. But I won't do it."

"What happened?"

"I did everything for that man. I mean everything.
Even his household chores. I took his dirty laundry
to the cleaners, did the food shopping, all of that.
I was his nurturing confidant, besides my actual
duties at the job."

"Okay. And?"

"Well, all the while he was making passes at me.
Asking me out. Pressuring me, ya know?"

"Uhm-hmm. And?"

"And, I wouldn't do it. I mean, I know all about
his past. The girl who worked for him before me—
she left a note in my desk, cussing his ass out. The
note told the whole story. Not only that, I also juggled different girls he was seeing. I told lies to keep
him out of trouble."

"Okay, so . . . we're talkin' screenplay here. Or a
soap opera. What's the bottom line?"

She couldn't tell what was on my mind, but so far
her boss was batting 700 as far as I was concerned. I
envied him for having had a woman so devoted to
his concerns. But apparently, he let a good thing go,
I thought.

"I needed to go. I need to be where I'm appreciated. And I thought of you."

*Read my mind, girl; you'll see just how I'd like to appreciate you.*

"I'm flattered, but what could you do for me?" I figured I'd start by having her beg and work her way up.

"Well, for one, you've got a great business. You deal with many different artists, whereas, at the label, I just worked with a few. Very limited potential for growth. I also like this environment. And you'll probably be a better boss than Stewart was."

"How about a trial run? I'll pay your train fare for a month or two—maybe a few other expenses— until you settle in. You've got to substantiate in value what I give to you in dollars. The only way for me to get an idea of your work is for you to start with probation. If things change, if your performance brings added convenience, then this could work. More convenience isn't *all*, Deidra. You'll have to contribute ideas and inspire projects here. We only survive by bringing in money. No money, we don't exist."

Deidra was all nods. She agreed to everything, and I suddenly had a new assistant. She worked overtime. Cleaned up where cleaning was required. Made me coffee and answered my phones. She kept the interns motivated and dressed provocatively enough that I'd find myself staring at her behind. When she was in the bathroom, I invaded her purse and personal items. Flipped through her bank statement book, her organizer, and her checkbook. She kept a tampon and a bit of makeup in her purse, and had a rabbit foot attached to her house keys. I noticed that her finances were stretched to their limits. That she paid the phone and electric bills piecemeal, never in full. There was a low bank balance. Her journal lauded me as the person she most wanted to be like. Her notes built me up as a king on a throne—a man she'd do anything for. The most obvious note read: *"I can't believe I'm here. His assistant! SHIT! I'm the woman—next to the man. I thought I'd never get myself into this position again . . . swore to it. But this is different altogether. All he has to do is say the word and I'll drop my pants. No questions asked."* The entry in her organizer was dated and initialed.

I heard Deidra coming back and I rushed to return to my desk. As if I didn't just see her naked through her possessions. When she came back in the loft I swiveled around in my chair to watch her. I studied her closely. She was a busy bee until she realized I was looking at her from across the floor.

"What?" she said with a girlish chuckle.

"You don't mind if I watch you, do you?"

"I . . . guess not." She looked at me as if I had swallowed stupid pills all of a sudden. She tried to go back to what she was doing, but finally said, "Okay, I give up. Could you tell me *why* you're staring at me?"

Being one who doesn't pass on certain opportunities, I said, "I'm starting to agree with you. I'm agreeable with everything about you, as far as I can see."

Her eyes shifted away, and then back to me. Deidra gave this sort of fawning expression that was more submissive than exaggerated.

"Come 'ere," I told her.

She did, in a pace that was slower than business-as-usual. My posture was atrocious; I slouched in my chair with my legs open. Douglass, the Svengali.

Deidra stopped at a safe distance, but was close enough to take my hand when I put it out. Maybe she thought I wanted her to help me up, because she attempted to pull. But I was stronger. I tugged her closer to where she stood between my legs, and then I pulled downward so that she had no choice but to kneel. Staring up at me with the most abandon I'd ever seen, Deidra's glassy eyes begged for understanding; except I took it the way I wanted—the way "the Captain" would see it. The silence waned as I penetrated her eyes with my own.

"Do you want—" she began.

"Shhhh . . . quiet," I cut her off, and she complied. After a moment or so, once I felt her uneasiness, I leaned in with my head a touch away from hers, whispering into her ear. I could hear her breathing . . . it was warm on my collar.

"You okay?"

Deidra didn't speak . . . she simply nodded.

"Remember when I spoke about you adding value?"

"Uhm-hmm."

"Well, I just had an idea," I whispered. "From the moment I first saw you I liked you. I knew you were the bomb, and that by any means necessary, you'd be mine—one way or another."

I didn't let her see my lying eyes. Our cheeks were still close as peach fuzz to a peach.

"So here you are, part of my world. I thought I'd ask you something . . . *May I?*"

"The suspense is killing me. Please, ask me." Deidra sounded as though she might be hyperventilating.

"Okay. You've been with guys before, haven't you?"

"A . . . a couple."

"A couple . . . Does that mean five, ten, twenty?"

"*No!* Like . . . three."

"So you've fucked three guys?"

Deidra took a second, then said, "Yes."

*Good*, I considered, happy to get sex into the conversation.

"Have you . . . done *other* things with these guys?"

"I . . . guess. It depends what you mean."

"Deidra . . . look at me. And don't lie to me. Did you suck their dicks?"

She hesitated, then looked down while answering, "Just two of 'em."

"Was that recently?"

"About a year ago."

"Did you swallow?"

Deidra's eyes widened, not believing that I was so straightforward. So abrupt and crass.

"Probably, a couple of times."

My imagination was spinning ideas now. I took another look at her—specifically, her lips. Then I dug into her eyes before I sat back in my seat and looked in my lap. I decided not to say another word. Deidra finally put her hands on top of my thighs while looking up at me. She started to talk again, but

I put my finger to her lips. She rubbed my thighs, building some confidence for herself. Her hands eased to my zipper, slowly pulling it down. I was as large as ever in my pants, and I never took my eyes off of her—looking for any sign of dissension. She freed the slave and looked it over, studying it. But my gaze didn't cower. I merely clasped my hands together and propped my chin on top of my fists. She looked back down and lowered her head—first smoothing the head of my stiff muscle against her cheek (getting to know me better, I suppose) and then kissing it until she took me between her lips. Her eyes were closed now. I was delirious with joy, still observing her buildup and the friction she served with her lips, tongue, and hand.

"Use both hands, sweetheart . . . that's a girl." I used "girl," "sweetheart," and "baby" now to guide her. I learned a few women ago that when they're submitting they like to be treated as subservient. Depends on the mood, I guess.

It was crazy how one moment, this was the all-knowing assistant, who was sharp as nails and took no shit from anybody, the next, she's sucking me off like a vacuum with a pretty face. I just sat back and enjoyed this.

*Suck it, baby. And swallow, too. That's added value I'm talkin' about, baby.*

# Chapter 12
## ANGEL

**H**i, Angel. It's Dougie."

I took a deep breath, my eyes fluttered, and then I answered, "I was hoping you would call."

"Why?"

"Why? You so funny, Douglass."

"But I wasn't joking. I wish you could see my face. Tell me why, Angel. *Why* did you hope I'd call?"

He wasn't obnoxious about it, just wanted to get deep in my head, I suppose. I just loved his sexy voice, but didn't say it to him.

"Well, because I'm in New York and I wanted to see you."

"Okay. I'll go for that."

"Oh—you—are—just a barrel of laughs, Mister *SuperStar.*"

"Speaking of which, congratulations. I saw that your single went to number one on the pop charts and the album is still movin' up too. It's got a bullet."

"Thanks. I don't really pay attention to all that stuff, ya know."

"You'd better, baby. Miss Reachin' for Double Platinum."

I blushed, not because he praised my album sales, but because he called me *baby* for the first time. I sighed, wondering when I'd see him again and if he'd kiss me on the mouth this time.

"I'm rehearsing tomorrow at SRO. It's on fifty—"

"I know where it is. I sat in on Redman's session there once. Caught a contact too."

"A contact?"

"Oh . . . never mind," he said. "I'll be there. What time?"

"We start at eight in the morning."

"Bet. I'll bring the coffee and donuts."

"They're gonna have all that there, silly."

"I know. It was just a figure of speech. Actually, *I'm* the coffee and donuts."

"Oooo—kay. Sounds delicious. See ya!"

Why does Doug strike me as *so damn sexy*? He really is a lot of fun to talk to and to be with. I'm so comfortable around him. I was groggy, grumpy, and I swear I felt a cramp on rehearsal day. My period was due in a couple of days. I was hoping it wouldn't come early. I drank loads of orange juice, praying that it wouldn't come. Douglass showed up with a girl at his side. I hadn't seen her the first couple of times Doug and I were together, but somehow she looked familiar. I know she couldn't be his girlfriend or wife or nothin'. 'Cause he wouldn't be on me so tight—the flowers, the cards, and the phone calls. Still, I couldn't help but wonder.

"Mother . . . come. I want you to meet someone."

"All right, baby, but you've gotta go back to work in a minute. They're going over choreography next," she warned as we walked over to welcome him.

"Hi, Douglass. I wanted you to meet my mother. Mother, this is the man I told you runs *SuperStar*; remember the cover story they did on me? The magazine I showed you?"

"Of course, dear. And how are *you*, sir?"

"Please, everybody calls me Douglass or Doug. Dougie if you're a close friend," he said to Mother with a straight face and all. I swore my heart was gonna fall into my stomach if he said anything too personal. I was ready to kill him if he did.

"Well, okay then, Dougie. And this is?"

"Of course, silly me. This is Deidra, my new assistant. Deidra, this is Angel's mother and this is the lovely Angel whom I've told you so much about."

I shook hands with the girl. We looked like two kittens touching paws. I also tried to catch a vibe— the way we women like to do. Like an investigation.

*Okay! Did you screw him?!* I wanted to ask, but my smile was fixed on my face. And Mother was monitoring everything.

Shatima was in charge of my dance moves. I was okay with some moves, but others were just a bit much; too funky for my taste. I like to concentrate on singing. Besides, I know from the last video— where I made mostly hand moves and wiggled my body—that folks more or less expect that in my live performances. So the less dance steps, the better. But I swear, some of the stuff Shatima did was so sexy, and I know I don't have to sing, just lip sync over and over again while they shoot the video. I've watched Whitney's videos like a billion times and the only two where she's really gettin' down is "I Wanna Dance with Somebody" and "So Emotional."

Even then, she's really only jumpin' up and down. I can't lie, I study Whitney 'cause that's who I wanna be like. Not look like her or think how she does, I'm my own woman. But I study her as a model. I study her success. To watch her is to go to class; Singing Success 101. I watch her mannerisms and the facial expressions on stage—how she controls the crowd. Her performance and vocals are so rich. And she's always in control. I guess you get comfortable after so many shows. I'm sure she's done hundreds by now. I'm only in my sixties with live performances, Times Square should be number sixty-six with all the work I'm doing for the video.

**A**fter lunch, Mother went back to the hotel and I had a chance to speak with Douglass alone.

"She works with you, huh?"

"Good work, too," he said.

*No he did not lick his lips!*

Then he said, "Why? You jealous?"

*What in the—* I started to get an attitude real quick. I was about to tell him off and the whole nine. But he had this smile that said he was kidding me.

"Relax, I'm only playing. She does office work, Angel. Answers phones, inventory. She keeps it clean. Polishes things. Makes things real convenient for me. Allows me to do better work, more efficiently."

I was looking over at his assistant the whole time. She was across the lobby kickin' it with one of my dancers. I guess I did kinda step out there.

"So what's up?"

"You! Damn, baby. Did you come up or what? I must've counted thirty dancers. Shatima's moves are *like that* and with your pretty face in the middle of it all? I smell another platinum single."

"I hope so. You think?"

"I *know*. You . . ." He took this deep breath, like air was coming from deep down in his gut. ". . . you make me *so* proud. Proud to know you . . . proud to be in your company. Just plain proud, girl."

I swear I wanted to just throw my arms around him at that second—but like fifty people were around us. And I know they were already nosy and wondering.

"Can we go somewhere quiet?"

"I'll step away, you follow. Studio B . . . they went out for lunch."

Now it was time for *my* deep breath. I was suddenly the center of attention, like *everybody* was looking at me. Or maybe I was just imagining things. But one thing I know is I was sweatin' something special. I strolled back in the studio where our soundstage was, grabbed a towel, and headed over to studio B all casual, like nothing was going on. The studio was dark. Just a little light from fixtures on the walls. I passed an engineering booth to find the lobby.

"Where you goin'?"

He scared the mess out of me. Grabbed me. Spun me around. And I was suddenly in his embrace. Had my arms pinned to my sides. My heart started beating again once I realized I wasn't about to be raped. We were still for a second. I could feel my eyes gettin' glassy and I let him take over. I'm no pro at kissing, but I had a little experience and of course I was steady watchin' Brucilla and Macolm, kissin' all heavy and stuff—on *The Young & the Restless*. Father says that those shows are too suggestive, and that the writers are responsible for life imitating art. He says there are legions of followers who watch the soaps and try to mold their own relationships after the stories. But I say, it's situations like this, those compromising times, when a girl's gotta have some type of ruler to go by. What's too little or too much?

Douglass was gentle with me. I inhaled his cologne as my oxygen and his own scent as my nourishment. His tongue was so juicy—his lips so authoritative. I was under a spell. I wasn't anywhere *near* thinking about my horror story with Sincere. As far as I was concerned, I was somewhere on the other side of the planet, experiencing my own pleasure principle. I fed Doug my tongue, and he ate me like a hungry man. All the while, he pulled me up against him, making me warm and even moister between my legs.

"Sorry . . ." He stopped. "I must've lost my mind."

My breathing was like a shiver in the snow. I put my arms around his neck and looked dead in his eye. I saw Jada do this once in *Jason's Lyric*.

Then I said, "Could you manage to lose your mind once again?" The moment was so timeless. The pleasure, so painfully limited. I felt as if I was caught in a web of wonder . . . wondering where I was and wondering where I was going. When he pulled away from me and the kissing melted into thin air, there was this deadly silence. I swallowed in the absence of knowing what to say or do, as he gazed into my soul through my eyes.

"You'd better get back out there. There're millions of dollars counting on you."

"Yeah. Crazy, ain't it? Us foolin' around back here while all those folks are working for li'l ol' me."

I didn't expect to giggle and act all girlish and shy, but I did. I turned around and rushed out to the lobby. Tried to act natural, like my panties *weren't* soaked when they sure were.

# Chapter 13
## DOUGLASS

It got to the point that everywhere I turned, every magazine I picked up, and every channel I flipped to was about her. I know I wasn't falling for the girl. Or was I? Damn, she's fine. I can't dwell on her age 'cause it'd make me crazy to *not* have Angelica somewhere in my life. That day at SRO studios was so fucking mind-blowing. My dick got hard as stale French bread, all pressed up against Angel like that. I wondered if she knew how excited I was. I wondered if she even knew *what* an erection was in the first place. After the rehearsal, I couldn't avoid Deidra's questions. I think she was jealous, but I wasn't about to hide shit. I keeps it real.

"Look," I told her in the car. "You're my assistant. You're right in the thick of things, where it counts. I'm making more money now, paying your ass real good and don't I lay it on you right? Huh?" I was demanding and imposing; I wouldn't accept anything but the answer I wanted and the fantasy I designed.

"Yes. You *do* do that. I just . . . I just don't see why you have to be with . . . everybody. *I* want to be everybody for you."

"Deidra . . . we discussed this before. Why are you going back there? Huh? Why can't you find happiness in the space I've given you? You've got a part of my world. What? You changed your mind? Not happy with all I'm giving you? *Huh?*" I let myself get all worked up. We were just entering the down ramp to take the Major Deegan Thruway back to New Rochelle. I could feel my skull fuming. I pulled over.

"Okay. Get the fuck out."

Deidra looked at me with distressed eyes. Then at the traffic down on the Deegan. It was getting dark. Rush hour. She looked back at me. Tears forming. Voice cracking, she said, "I'm sorry, Dougie. Please. I'm sorry. You're right . . ."

"Yeah, you sorry *now* 'cause your ass is left out on the street. I don't wanna hear it. Get the fuck out. Out! *Now!*"

The tears were falling. "But where do I go? What do I do?" she asked frantically.

"I don't care whatcha do—or where you go. I *do* know you need to get the *fuck* out of my car!"

She started to get out. Sobbing all the while.

"And you need to find a new job while you're at it. *Bitch!*"

Deidra closed the door so soft I wasn't sure if it was closed all the way. She stood outside of the car, hands to her face, like a naked lamb. I slammed my foot down on the accelerator, leaving a cloud of dust around her. Halfway down the ramp I hit the brakes and felt a slight skid. I could see her in the rearview mirror, my brake lights glowing on her—an outline amid the wafting dust and smog.

I smiled. Then I beeped the car horn once—
quick.

Again—two times, quick.

Deidra trotted down to where the car was, her
arms swinging and her body working hard to balance on her high heels. When she got back in the
car, I put the car in park—for emphasis—and I
faced her. A car was easing down the ramp behind
me; its horn sounded.

"Did you say you're sorry?"

She nodded excitedly, wiping away the tears.

"Say it like you mean it."

"I AM SO SORRY, Dougie. I will keep my mouth
shut from now on. I don't know why I said anything,
because I'm so happy with you. I can't imagine
what I'd do without you, without being part of your
world . . ."

She shifted over across the front seat and got
close enough to kiss me. I turned my lips away and
let her kiss me on the cheek.

"Will you forgive me, Dougie? Please, Dougie?
I'll do anything for you."

"Anything?"

"Everything and anything."

I took the car out of park and pulled to the shoulder of the exit. The three or four cars behind me
sped by, sounding their horns in a fit of rage. My car
was back in park now.

"First of all, take off those stupid shoes. I like you
barefoot."

"I know . . ." She quickly undid them. "But that's
usually in the office."

I'm thinking *shuddup*. She had them off now.

"The car, the office, whatever . . . it's all my house." I depressed the button on the door panel and the front seat slowly eased back—making more room. "I don't think you've begged enough. I want to see the whole act—the begging, the pleading, the tears, *all of it*. Make me a fuckin' believer."

Deidra took a deep breath and began filling my head with a bunch of accolades. *You're the best this . . . you're the greatest that . . . I love this . . . I love that . . . I'll never . . .* So on and so forth. I had to stop her.

"Shuddup, Deidra. Just shut the fuck up. No—no . . . leave the tears. I like *them*. But what I want you to do right now is open your shirt . . . lemme see those itty-bitty titties you got."

I knew that the mention offended her, she was so self-conscious about her small chest. I've seen this before—her unbuttoning the blouse, unsnapping the bra. They weren't any bigger than tennis balls. And sagging a little, too. This was the best, the most submissive I've ever seen her. It dwarfed that fuckin' ego of hers, but inflated my own demented fantasies. The office was one thing indeed, but these instances were becoming more and more crazy. More neurotic and whimsical, to say the least—at a thruway on an exit ramp for Christ's sake. She sat there now, top open, her chest exposed for passing cars to maybe get a peek at.

"Good . . . good," I muttered as I turned up WBLS on the car stereo. The Brothers Johnson were singing "Strawberry Letter 23" as I leaned back with my hand and arm extended over her headrest.

"Now let's get familiar. *Real* familiar."

Deidra's tear-soaked face lowered to my lap and during rush hour, in the most obscure, yet high-profile spot in New York, she sucked me 'til I was spent and she was thirst-quenched. Good ol' Deidra.

That evening with Deidra kept me busy for a few hours, and I didn't get back to Angel for a while. I eventually stopped by the video shoot, figuring it might teach me some things I could use for my own knowledge in television production. But that was all. Nothing beat an experienced woman; and Deidra sure knew how to keep me happy. I was actually grateful to her for all she went through to satisfy my wild whims. The ass-smacking sessions of hot sex were keeping her happy too. So, it wasn't necessarily the one-way satisfaction it seemed to be. It got to the point where I had to scold her for calling me *"Daddy"* one day with an intern present. I'm sure the intern didn't hear. But it was close enough for me to hold a li'l conference with Deidra.

It was times like those when I'd pop her in the head. I'd be playful about it, but firm enough to make myself clear. "You have to keep certain things separate from the others," I'd tell her. Eventually, she'd promise not to let it slip again and that she'd tighten up her act.

Deidra was so devoted, even telling me about all of Angel's phone calls. She even got to know our situation more from a relationship counselor's point of view, and also told Angel things to console her when she felt alone.

"You got that girl strung out, Douglass. She's definitely hooked on you." Since Dee knew the deal I had her play cupid when necessary. She got into long telephone discussions with Angel, and encouraged her wherever possible. It sure pays to have a woman doing the talking for you. It's like having an inside man at a bank to keep the vault open for easy access. And I wasn't stupid; I told Dee that if I even *sense* Angel letting up, that I'd kick her ass. Then I'd toss her out on it. For now, I was satisfied with making brief calls and complimenting Angel on her latest successes. After all, she was steady living in LA with her mother and father. What was she gonna do, stop by for a booty call?

In the meantime, Deidra was becoming one of my biggest resources, organizing my office, collecting on the ad space we sold, and setting up my television interviews as usual. She scheduled some big ones too. Fat Joe, Mary J. Blige, Nancy Wilson, MC Lyte, Chaka Khan, Brian McKnight, and many others. She was on a roll, focused, and unimpressed with all the celebrities and their fame. She handled them like a Wall Street tycoon would a hostile takeover, merely wanting to serve my best interests. I swear if it weren't for her insecurities and the way our relationship jumped off, I might consider marrying that girl.

Deidra also relocated from Jersey to New Rochelle, where I arranged for her to stay in a two-bedroom apartment above the copy shop on the corner. I paid the rent and furnished it too. Douglass, the sugar daddy.

Things got so good with the magazine—now near 128 pages, with half as many pages of advertisement—that I decided on a move to Main

Street. It was a leap out of the shadows, the hide-away feel of the loft, and the industrial zone in which we had to make due. On Main Street, I could claim credibility and all things substantial. We were now *official*, so to speak. The rent was a little more, but I had a second-floor office that had a wall-sized window overlooking Main Street. There was a re-ception area and a common area where interns and salespeople were stationed, as well as room for four desks, a large leather couch, and a water ma-chine. I leased a number of computers for everyone to use, including a number of freelance writers and graphic designers who could come in to use them on their own schedules. The entire facility was car-peted, furnished with black leather couches and ac-cent lighting.

My own office was pimped out, with a framed Herb Ritts photograph of a proud and topless Naomi Campbell with her perfect tits, bearskin rugs on the floor, a thirty-inch monitor suspended up high from the wall across from my oversized desk, and a plethora of Afrocentric books, sculptures, and in-door plants. I kept the loft as I would my own living quarters, and managed, finally, to separate my per-sonal life from my work environment when neces-sary.

We had new faces, which complimented our *Su-perStar* world, including Maureen, who was the young, tall one with the baby fat, big breasts, and Jell-O ass. Where the average intern simply sat through an interview with me (in Naomi's company), Maureen sang for me on demand. It was another way for me to see her naked. She felt uncomfortable with calling me by my first name, and always called me Mr. Douglass. That's like calling Eddie Murphy, Mr. Eddie. Just plain ignorant youth. But I didn't mind. As long as she kept doing the menial stuff like fetching my coffee, my lunch, and basically every other thing I asked for; as long as she maintained the subordinate, suck-up roll that answered to my whims, I was ever satisfied.

Sheena was another intern who began submitting stories and eventually became an assistant to Deidra. There were times when I had Sheena sit real close— so I could molest her with my eyes—and she'd take dictation for me. It got to the point where she'd know what I wanted to say and how. Always perky, with breasts that stood on their own and big black almond eyes against her desert sand complexion, Sheena was a girl I'd never get tired of looking at.

Phil was our resident white boy. I've known him since I was sixteen. His father owned the local Yamaha shop. When I bought my bike back in the day, he was the one who delivered it and then taught me the basics of riding. And we've been buddies ever since. He used to joke about his coming by the *SuperStar* offices in order to keep up with the goings-on in the black community. But I knew better. I knew that he was basically looking out for me. He'd taken a liking to me and wanted to make sure I succeeded. But in the meantime he became a club bouncer, then a bodyguard for local politicians, and I naturally hired him to run security for me when I promoted concerts. Phil had that disciplined look of a cop, but the freelance attitude of a bounty hunter.

He always had a nickel-plated .45 on his hip. Like this was Dodge City and he was Billy the Kid.

Reno was one of the later additions to the *Super-Star* family. The damned fool was playing with a pellet gun and ended up shooting himself in the eye. So one lid stays shut while the other eye works double time during all of his schemes and hustles. But I didn't see him as disabled when he came in to meet me. He was totally impressive and the missing eye was a handicap that I couldn't help but overlook. Reno's attitude fascinated me. He was hungry and insatiable. I was sold the moment he said he'd even get my coffee and newspapers on a volunteer basis until I thought he was worthy of a salary—words that were music to my ears.

Finally there was Miss Dotty, who came in with a vague resume, but a strong presence. She was the elder among us, at least thirteen years older, and even sold cars at one point in her life. She went on and on about all of the marvelous contacts she had and all of the businesses that would immediately buy ads in *SuperStar Magazine*, and how the state of black business would benefit tremendously by the influence of this powerful economic tool. *Sold*.

So then, being an inlet for information and resources, and also distributing such ideas in print and on cable TV, made the *SuperStar* team a welcome part of most any music business or community event or project. Madison Square Garden, The Beacon Theater, and Radio City Music Hall became our virtual home-entertainment systems, since we were invited to everything—every type of event and performance. The Grammy Awards, the ASCAP Awards, and the

MTV Awards became celebrations that we'd work our schedules around. Furthermore, the dozens of major and independent record labels and movie production companies we dealt with *always* had new products and events that needed to be introduced and promoted to viewers. Not to mention all the listening parties and movie premieres we attended, always with a heavy celebrity presence.

These exclusive events always promised impromptu performances, like the time Stevie Wonder started singing while Doug E. Fresh provided human beats. Or the times when DMX, Notorious B.I.G., or Foxy Brown freestyled without music. Or Phyllis Hyman joining in on Angela Bofill's performance. Or Wyclef taking the stage with every artist of every genre. Hip-hop was a robust culture that, thanks to the advent of video and the Internet, was becoming immensely popular. And with every maturing stage of the music industry's days and nights, our *SuperStar* crew was there to absorb it all and contribute to it all, from the inductions into the Hall of Fame to the backstage happenings. From the lines outside of the events to the VIP areas, *Super-Star* was a part of almost every sensational moment in time. And we never got tired. Nightclubs like Perk's and The Cotton Club in Harlem; The Shadow, Crobar, Club Show, Bentley's, and The City in midtown; and The Shark Bar, Chaz & Wilson's, Etiole, and Birdland farther uptown, were all second homes to me. They were stop-and-go's, which would fill in the voids between, before, or after the larger events. Each club had its own special atmosphere and a following that attracted fanatics, gold diggers, and plenty of eye candy.

I would glide right through the entrance with Phil (always serious and on alert) and Reno (a mere tag-along) beside me. We'd float past the line outside, and then through the crowd indoors, until we'd find ourselves in the VIP area of the club. The three of us always traveled with that "don't start none, won't be none" attitude, and we always got the respect I'd earned from years in the entertainment business. So naturally I was tight with Frank Horne, Birdland's promoter. It was during one of our outings at Birdland that Frank would introduce me to my next employee.

"This is Jo-Jo, and Jo-Jo, this here's Douglass. He runs *SuperStar*. He's got a TV show, a magazine, and everything."

I knew Frank wasn't as much a fan of my show as, say, a weekly viewer might be, but he knew just enough to make those introductions that kept him so connected in the important social circles.

I shook hands with the petite woman Frank introduced me to, and I passed her a magazine that we always kept for just these purposes. *SuperStar*, for me, had become my business card, and it worked just as well.

"Yeah, Doug, I was just telling her about you a while ago, and here you are. What a coincidence."

I wondered what Frank was up to, because I hadn't been in the spot for more than ten minutes, and already Frank was passing me this attractive piece of ass. I also didn't miss how comfortable she seemed in the VIP lounge, sipping on some bubbly with her big glassy eyes. Skeptical, I flashed Frank a look of wonder before I pulled him aside.

"What gives?" I asked him. Everybody knew Frank was married to that fine-ass *Essence* model, so I took a stab at what his dilemma might be, guessing that this chick was a nuisance, and that maybe he was trying to get rid of her. Or maybe it's just my lyin' eyes that were coming up with all these ideas.

"She's just a friend," Frank said. "Just a friend."

"Then how come she's all up on you like that? Frank, I ain't no fool. *Somethin'* must be going on."

"Doug, I'm bein' straight up with you. It's not like that . . ."

"You never hit it?"

"Nope. I'm married, dude. I don't want no trouble. The girl needs a friend. She's in college and wants to get in entertainment, so I told her I'd introduce her to some people. And you the man."

I cut my eyes at Frank trying to figure out if he was just talkin' shit and if I was right for putting on my Timb boots that evening; preparation for the bullshit he might be feeding me. But Frank didn't give in. And besides, Jo-Jo wasn't the baddest-looking chick in the club.

Later, Jo-Jo and I talked.

"I like this. You did it all by yourself?" Jo-Jo said while flipping through the latest copy of *SuperStar Magazine*.

"Not exactly. But I started it from scratch and built a company around it and it grew like a wild orchid."

"Mmmm . . . I *love* orchids. They're beautiful."

Jo-Jo was growing on me, quick. She had long black hair, a Dominican accent under her clear English, she was shapely and petite, and from what I could see her curves were stretching the potential of some ugly, copper-brown mesh halter top that exposed some of her midsection and navel. Her exotic hips must've loved the mauve silk side-tie skirt that reached down to her ankle-laced sandals. But it wasn't the mismatched gift wrapping that intrigued me about Jo-Jo; it was her eyes. Something in those eyes that was greater than mere desire reached out to me. Something better than Deidra's energy or Angel's music. Or maybe it was just my weakness for attractive young women. Who knows? In any event, I told her, "You *are* the orchid."

She looked down, humbled by my compliment and then shifted her weight to the opposite leg.

"Thank you," she said. We chatted some more, nursing our drinks, pondering, listening, and lingering amid throngs of jazz enthusiasts.

"Do you guys offer internships?" she asked.

"*Do* we? I probably have twenty interns. All young women in college. Like you."

"Yeah? Where's your office?"

"Up in New Rochelle. About thirty minutes away."

"Can I see it?"

She was quick with the questions and ideas, giving me little time to think. I looked at my watch. It was pushing up on one in the morning.

"You can see it now if you want."

Half of me wanted to touch her; the other loved

devoted workers and impulsive, affirmative action. All the while, I thought hard about having both.

I dropped off Reno and Phil, both of them smiling behind Jo-Jo's back. It was the most dubious of circumstances for me to have a companion in the Jeep on the way back home. Like the half dozen times before, it was obviously the beginnings of a one-night stand.

I gave her that exclusive tour of *SuperStar*'s headquarters, and by 3 A.M. I came up with the cockamamie idea of taking photos. And Jo-Jo went right along with the program. We took it to the middle of Main Street, where there was no traffic on a clear windless night. I played photographer, ordering various poses, stepping in to manually fix her positions, keeping things provocative. Right there on the blacktop.

"Now gimme that sassy pose you Spanish girls like to do, with the attitude and the hand on the hip. Okay, now turn your back to me and put both hands on your hips, thumbs forward, legs spread . . . that's right—that's *right*. Now bring your head back, more to the left. Like you're looking up at the moon. Yup—gotcha. *Gotcha!*" Her ass was gleaming under the moon.

"Okay. Now take one hand and grab a bunch of hair and lift it up. Hold it at the top of your head. Yup. That's it. *That's it*. Beautiful. Now spin around. Gimme your sexiest look. Let your hair go wild— over your face. *Yeah, baby!* Now bring both arms up, like you're laying in bed and he's stretching those hands back to the headboard. Oh, yeah! Straight sex, baby! That's it!" I had Jo-Jo stretch that pretty ass of hers in a hundred different positions—the whole Simon Says bit—and I *still* wasn't satisfied. In one pose she even bent over to look at me between her legs. And it was then that I knew her ass was mine and that the camera was merely the catalyst to get me there.

# Chapter 14
## ANGEL

**D**ouglass never came to LA like he said he would. He had me waiting for him, too. All open and moist like a fresh cherry pie with a slice missing. But he made up for it by calling me and sending me three dozen roses for my seventeenth birthday and promising me the world when we got together again. I didn't need much more to get over it since it was time to head to New York again. The label decided to make something big of this visit, bigger than just a measly television special. So they set up a big birthday bash for me, even though my seventeenth birthday was at least two weeks behind me. Besides the birthday party, I just shot the pilot for my own sitcom—*ANGELIQUE*—that a major network made a bid for. Lianne tells me that getting picked up is a sure thing when networks start fighting over your pilot. When the third music video came out, a remix with a few other major female rappers making cameo appearances, my album suddenly shot to triple platinum. Lianne was getting offers like crazy. The label execs say that my first project was a one-in-a-million shot and that debuts usually don't go multiplatinum. So the big success called for more meetings with Mom and I in the days leading up to the party. To say the least, I was caught up in the whole hurricane of interest. And there were plenty of reasons to celebrate. I was Angel, the "it girl" of the moment. There were endless TV interviews, more magazine covers, and now, Revelor Cosmetics wanted to hire me as a spokesperson. Mother set things up with three different publicists to handle media—one from the television industry to handle all the TV interviews on the networks and cable, an LA-based publicist to handle the radio and Internet forums, and a third New York-based publicist to take care of magazines and newspapers and such. Of course Lianne, my girl, was the one in charge of the birthday bash itself. But these other three ladies combined were responsible for luring top celebrities and personalities, as well as setting up press runs in just about every media source in the country. Lianne was excited about it all because, she says, it all would help get more records sold, and set me up for my sophomore album.

To add icing to the cake, I'm friends with a lot of models now. Whether they're fair-weather types or not, I don't know. But since things have blown up so much, the new friendships never stopped coming. Sometimes I just go with the flow. I trust folks until they give me a reason not to. Of course Mother tells me to trust no one until they give you reason to do so. Damn, our generations are so ass-backward.

The night of my birthday bash was amazing. That LA publicist set it up so that Kara and Veronica (also Revelor models) and I would arrive together at my party like a Revelor trio. We left my hotel room all silly and dressed in black velvet, satin, and silk evening gowns, all smellin' like wildflowers. Cleavage was *everywhere*. Plus, Kara had me trippin' in the limo, showing me how to keep myself perky for the cameras. Veronica added her two cents too, saying, "Girlfriend, it's all about the nipples. Trust me. More cleavage is out. That was *last* year. *This* year, you've gotta have a pretty face, some cleavage, and *nipples*."

Those two had me hollerin' all the way to the party. The most down-to-earth women I've ever met. And I've been around lots of celebs, but I think supermodels are the coolest because they've been all over the world, virtually naked. I mean, the *world* has seen them in underwear, imagined them in less, and dreamed of being with them. But up close, they're like, the craziest. I'd swear *they* were the ones to see the *world* naked.

"Okay, ladies, we're here!" Kara announced. "Now, let me share some insider stuff with you. Liz, my publicist, gave me the hot 'n' juicy."

I was listening to Kara, but looking at the front of the House of Billiards. Even though it was a great big facility with dozens of pool tables inside, the outside was set up like a big movie premiere at the Manns Theater in Hollywood: big spotlights searching the dark sky, red carpet from the entrance to the curb; velvet ropes, fans, and loads of paparazzi.

"She says that both Tysons will be there. The one who can't keep his hands off, and the fine one who you don't *want* to keep his hands off. She says don't be intimidated by the thugs—and smack their hands if they try to touch you." Even as she spoke, we were laughing so hard that tears started forming.

"Well, I see Nitro, so I won't have any problems with that," I told them.

"Who's Nitro?"

"The big one in the tux; blue cummerbund."

"Oooh well, Mr. Café au lait!" said Veronica before she licked her lips like she saw a candied apple.

"Don't mind her, Angelica. She'd freak the pants off of the Pope."

"Oooohhh, chile!" The air was stuck up in my lungs.

"Yeah, but I'd turn his ass out too, and then I'd be livin' in the Vatican. Runnin' shit!" We screamed bloody Mary and my ears almost went deaf.

"You ain't nuthin' nice, V." I wagged my head.

Just outside of the velvet ropes, Nitro opened the door and two other male escorts followed his lead as they helped us from the limo. The publicists stood by with clipboards pressed to their chests, waiting to give us all kinds of directions. It was like walking into a swarm with everyone's eyes pointing at you like stingers. Camera flashes were blinding us as our names were called out from every which way. Of course each of us has been here before, at the awards shows and premieres 'n' stuff. But this time, it was *all* about me. Every bit of it, like a coming-out event. And I can't lie; even though I felt sucked in and consumed by all of the attention, I loved every bit of it.

Once we stepped inside, there was applause so great it was overwhelming, like we were being swallowed by it. The whole party atmosphere blasted us, with pink and red balloons filling the air like billowing clouds of color. There were reception tables where folks signed in and received a hand stamp. We just bypassed all of that. In the meantime, Lianne was telling me something about photos but I hardly paid attention. I was too caught up in all the hoopla, the faces, the smiles, the cheerful eyes. LL Cool J's music was pumpin' and thumpin' somewhere in the rear, and it all made me wanna just shake my hips. Veronica was already shakin' her hips, arms all up in the air like a party animal.

*They're jinglin' baby / go 'head baby!*
*They're jinglin' baby /go 'head baby!*

Kara and I just smiled at each other. A couple of TV cameras came out of nowhere, with their counterparts stretching microphones at us over the velvet ropes. I think I heard Funkmaster Flex's voice over the music. He was keepin' things hype.

"Hi, baby!" Shatima strutted across the carpet—some kind of fashion model herself—and gave me the cheek-to-cheek kiss.

"Ooh girl, you just Miss Thang tonight, ain't you!"

I thanked her and struck a pose, playing up for still photos and TV cameras. More and more partiers gravitated toward us as Nitro pushed through. Nitro, the bulldozer. Lianne whispered to me that *SuperStar* was here and I lit up like nuclear radiation. Nobody else knew this, but my folds tremored. I flashed a suspicious eye at Lianne, wondering just how much she knew about my personal relations. I'd have to yell at her later, 'cause flowers were just showin' up in the *darnedest* places. Douglass just had too much access to be a li'l ol' New York entrepreneur.

Was it me? Or were all of us squinting in front of all those flashes and spotlights? We got sick of posing and went on to chat among ourselves. If the press people only knew how bad we talked about them behind their backs. Meanwhile, Lianne brought over a plate of goodies. Shrimp, crackers and cheese, strawberries and cherries. Veronica is stupid, because she took a cherry and turned her back to the cameras so only Kara and I could see her do tricks with her tongue.

"Girl, you are just no good!"

"I told you, Angelica. Stay away from her, she'll get you in plenty of trouble."

"Don't hate, Kara. Try it, you might like it."

"Hey, I wanna mingle in the crowd a little."

"Uhm-hmm, and perhaps run into someone? Someone in *particular*?" suggested Veronica.

I said, "Girl, watch your mouth."

I kidded her with a soft punch and proceeded down the back steps to where I could get to the dance floor. Lianne caught up with me as Nitro led the way.

"They're gonna be singing 'Happy Birthday' to you soon, Angel. Don't wanna get lost in the party."

"Lianne, you need to stay with me so I don't get carried away out there. I'm gonna do this quick interview for *SuperStar*."

"Okay. Oh, by the way. Happy birthday. Again."

"Thank you. Again."

"One more thing, Angel . . ."

"What's up?"

"A couple of the NUBIANs are here."

"Is *that* so? Pray tell, Lianne," I said as I came to a sudden stop on the stairs. "Which NUBIANs would they happen to be?"

I put my hand on my hip, knowing that she could've planned this all along, or that Sincere may have paid her off.

"Uhm, Dario?" she answered in a most embarrassed tone.

"Uh-huh, go on."

"And, uh, Sincere?"

With my hand flying to my forehead, trying to soothe a sudden headache, I told her, "Lianne, you and I are gonna have words later. And I swear it's gonna be *some*thing!" My tone was just beyond playful. Nitro was waiting at the bottom of the steps, watching as if Lianne was the enemy. As if she wasn't the one who hired him in the first place.

"Come on, Nitro, I'm ready to get my party on," I said.

Lianne straggled behind, fakin' like her clipboard was calling her.

# Chapter 15
## DOUGLASS

If there's one thing I've never done, it's to look at Darryl, with that broadcast video camera on his shoulder, and imagine that the lens is a portal to my audience. I don't see millions of people in their living rooms. I just see Darryl. And the spotlight.

"Welcome to Angel's big bash, Veronica! Long time, no see. Of course our viewers know you for your hosting *Sho-Nuff Fashion* on MTV, and your supermodel status in the *Sports Illustrated* swimsuit issue, and of course there's your work on Flex's latest mix tape. You've been quite the busy bee lately. How does one person find the energy to do so much?"

"I wake up!" She chuckled. "I just wake up with my dreams still intact, with my vision in focus. I'm simply driven and pulled by my passions."

We had to speak over the music, as they were playing Angel's song from the *Breathe* soundtrack, but I could hear every word as I leaned in, smelling her exotic fragrance.

"That's a wonderful message, Veronica. So tell me, what brings you out tonight?" I whipped the microphone back to Veronica's lips—those shiny, supple, delectable lips.

"I'm in total support of Angel. That's my *girl*, man. Anything she puts out—the songs, the TV shows, the makeup—when it comes out I'm right there to support it. One hundred percent!"

"Wow. That's a sister for you. Well, thank you for stopping by to talk to *SuperStar*. I see your party partner Kara here with you . . ."

"Hi, *SuperStar!*" Kara hopped up, throwing her arm around my neck. I put my own around her waist.

"Now you, sugar bear, have struck gold. You've got the movies . . . what, four of 'em since I last counted? You're in the Victoria bras, the hottest thing on *Oprah*. Fashion runways. Magazine covers. Is there ever gonna be an end to your power moves?"

"You know what, Doug? As much as I've been working, I really haven't been doing much more than being the best I can be. At whatever I do. But this thing isn't just about me. It's about the people before me. Iman, Beverly, and all the people after me. We've got to continue to support black content, black shows like yours, so that we can have more black images out there. If we keep laying the groundwork, there will be endless opportunities out there for girls like myself, like Veronica, and like Angel. We're only a few people, but there are millions of girls out there with beauty and potential. And unless there are vehicles out here to expose them, they'll never be seen . . ."

"True. True. So you've got to have more than a million in the bank right now."

"Well, a thousand, a million, a billion—*who's counting*? I don't really get into that. Angel is the girl tonight. This is her big birthday bash, all of the big names are here. I'm here to support my girl."

I realized Kara wanted to change the subject so I ran with it.

"How long have you known Angel?"

"Oh, for a while now. I feel like she's a sister. We always see each other at the awards and stuff. We did a spread in *Essence* together . . ."

"Oh, yes. I definitely saw *that* one."

"So now she's becoming a supermodel herself. She's already a super*star*; now she'll conquer the makeup world, and soon more TV and maybe movies too. No limit, baby! *No limit!!* " Kara shouted into the mic and did a little dance.

"Well, thank you for stopping by." I kissed her full on the cheek and she shuffled away, through the crowd behind Veronica. Deidra whispered in my ear to prepare me for the next interview. We were rollin' now. Almost eighteen interviews so far. Enough to use for at least ten one-hour segments. Content is key. The more the better.

"Finally, ladies and gentlemen, we're blessed and highly favored to have with us the *brother* of the birthday girl for the evening. Say hello to Angel's brother—Tray!

"Whassup, li'l man! You get to see big sis at home all day; you know, the usual routine. 'Sis! Can you PLEASE hurry up in the bathroom?' And 'Dag, Angel, you have to be on the phone ALL DAY!?' But now, you're out here in New York . . . it's a special day with a whole heap of special people around. Tell us, Tray, how much love you got for big sis?"

"Oh—I got maaad love for Angel. She hooked me up with a home studio so I can work on my own music. We go out all the time, shopping, movies, family picnics. It's all love."

As Tray shared the family jewels I conjured images in my mind to accompany his words.

"So no jealousy? Any fights you want to let us know about?"

"We're just human. Like every other brother and sister. Sure, we bug out on each other at times, but the bottom line is, we all gotta sit at the dinner table. We all gotta answer to Ma duke and Papa large. In the end, it's all love. That's my sister 'til I'm born again."

"So how big is this bash, dude?"

"Yo! I just met Funkmaster Flex! That's my *dawg!* And Red Alert's here, and I was play-fightin' with Mike Tyson. I don't care what nobody says. He's always gonna be the heavyweight champ of the world to me."

"So you've been busy tonight."

"Have I? I was just playin' pool, beatin' the pants off of LL Cool J and Latifah."

"Well, I'm gonna have to pull up on you later, champ. I got a few pool skills myself."

"Well, step up, dawg!"

Deidra again. I thanked Tray and he bounced away, rappin' to Meth and Mary's "You're All I Need." Now Angel was singing her way into the *SuperStar* spotlight.

"*You're all . . . I need . . . to get by . . . ooohaah . . .*"

As soon as Angel stopped, she ripped Mary's part of the song.

*"Like sweet mornin' dew . . . I took one look at you . . . and it was plain to see, you were my destiny!"*

"And here—she—is. The star of the evening! The pre-Madonna . . . the bubblin' brown sugar they call Angelica! Angel! Happy birthday from all of us at *SuperStar*!" I ignored her bodyguard.

"Thank you, sir. I appreciate all the love."

"So . . . how marvelous is all of this, Angel? Really."

"I'm just really blessed to get so much love . . ."

"And so much work!"

"Yeah . . . that too."

I was relieved that Angel was easy to talk to. After all, we hadn't been together for almost a year, ever since that delicious kiss at SRO studios. Of course we talked a lot on the phone. But seeing her, feeling her with my arm around her waist, and smelling her all up close was nothing more than a wake-up call. It stimulated my senses. Had me asking myself why I was trippin'. Why wasn't I hittin' that ass like it's never been hit?

"Okay, Angel, it's your night. Your moment. Millions of your fans are out there in TV land. They listen to your music, call into the stations, watch your videos, and soon they'll be watchin' you on your own sitcom while putting on makeup that you've endorsed. Talk to your people, Angel."

I handed her the microphone and I let Darryl the cameraman zoom in for a closeup. Exclusive words from Angel. I envisioned how the moment would look after I edited and laid graphics. "Angel-Vision," the TV would say.

"I . . . I really just want to thank all of you for supporting me through the years and I hope that you'll continue to watch and listen and want me as a contribution to your lives. I'm not perfect. Remember that. But hopefully, I can bring you some joy during your hard times and brighten your day just a little more during the good times . . ."

Angel's sincere words cut through the frivolity in the venue. I stood there, imagining her as my wife. Then she went on.

"There's something else I wanna tell you folks out there. This isn't easy. Sometimes being away from the ones you care about most is hard. It's worse than a bullet. And sometimes the pain makes you numb. I've been writing a lot of songs lately. One I've recently written hits home on my point. It's called 'Pain and Glory.' Some of the lyrics are as follows . . ."

Angel looked over at me—expressionless—and then back at the camera. I knew she'd be talking to me. I was glued to every sound.

> *It's the cost of living*
> *And there's no way to escape*
> *You have to stand the tests of time*
> *The choice is not even yours to make*
>
> *Girl, I know that it's hard*
> *You've had about as much as you can take*
> *But trust me when I tell you this,*
> *Troubles come, and troubles go away . . .*
>
> *The roses seem close enough to touch*
> *But believe me, girl, that's all made up*

*The truth is that you must feel pain to grow*
*That's a fact of life you should know*

*It's hard, yes, I know the story too well*
*These are times kept from age-old fairy tales*
*But time has answers too difficult to tell*
*Hold on, be strong, 'cause your glory will*
*   prevail . . .*

She handed me the mic and stepped up to kiss me on the cheek. Then she walked away. I was floored. I made the cut signal to Darryl, with my hand pretending to cut off my head. Deidra's sad eyes searched for my response to the testimony. I shook off the brush with reality. But all I could think was, *Yet another woman and more emotions to cope with.* All because of my endless, insatiable appetite for more.

It was written all over Deidra's face on the drive back to New Rochelle. But instead of my saying, *Here we go again,* I invited her comments.

"Okay. Cough it up. What's on your mind?"

"Nothin'."

"Deidra, it's *not* nothin'. There's something on your mind—let 'er rip."

"Whaddaya gonna do?"

"Would it hurt your feelings if I told you? Or do you just want me to assure you that things won't change between you and me?

"I don't think my feelings are an issue if you do assure me. At least I'll know *I'm* good. I mean, I'm handling my business, your business. Nothing's changed about that."

"Right."

"But then, you've got *her* feelings to think about. Do you really think she'll go for our *arrangement*? Think she can handle your lifestyle? It took *me* a while to settle. And I'm still here. I'm not going anywhere. But she's Miss Hollywood now. Every John will offer her his world *exclusively*. I don't think you can ever do that, player."

"You're right. I don't think I would give up my ways for some Pollyanna with a voice and a bank account. But I'll tell you what—just because she doesn't seem to be my type doesn't mean I'm not gonna try. You know me and persuasion are like night and day, you can't have one without the other."

"You gonna fuck her?"

"Ooh, maybe tomorrow. I'll stop by her hotel after work. Surprise her. Flowers. Gifts. You know the deal."

"I sure do. I sure do, Douglass."

"You gonna be all right?"

"Uhm-hmm." Deidra began to cry silent tears.

"Cheer up, girl. I'll give you somethin' to smile about when we get back."

"Uhm-hhm. Somethin' to fix everything, huh? *After.* That's always the answer."

"Huh . . ." I chuckled. "Well, isn't it?" I heard a deep breath.

Then she wagged her head before she said, "I don't know about it being the answer, but it sure eases the pain." Deidra slid over to lay her head against my shoulder. Then, with a slight smirk on her face she said, "Can I join you guys?"

"You mean like *Three's Company*?" Her smile emerged—the conspirator.

"Not on the first go-round, baby. I've gotta break her in first. You don't start *out* being freaky. It takes a minute."

"Never underestimate the power of freak in a female," she said.

And under my breath, I responded, "Ain't that a bitch."

# Chapter 16
## ANGEL

The party was a smash. Bigger than anything I've ever had. Bigger than anything I've ever been to. I couldn't avoid Sincere, though. He made sure to get my attention. It was just as my mother was about to start the singing of the birthday song up on stage with my brother, father, and industry folks on stage. Sincere shouted "Wait a minute!" He ran, jumped up on stage, and offered to lead the singing. I'm standing there on stage, petrified. Of course, nobody stopped him. He's only one of the biggest singers in the entire world. So he sings. I fawn. He steps up to kiss me after. I swear I coulda cut that boy with my eyes—daring him to come anywhere near my lips. He got the message. And so did *VIBE* magazine. They got hold of the photo and put it on the twenty-questions page. Question number one: *"Is it not obvious that Angel (the girl wonder) is finished with Sincere (of the super group NUBIAN)?"* Question two: *"Does it look like he's about to catch the most wickedest beat-down? Or are we just imagining?"*

The day after the event, I decided to shop a little. Nitro was really my bodyguard just for show, just for the party. But he decided on his own to stay with me.

He's kinda cute and all, but so big. Makes me wince just to think.

Anyway, we stopped by the Village where I bought some cute sunglasses and a couple of teddies to sleep in. One had bold white letters over the black silk that read BABE-A-LICIOUS. The other was aqua green (also silk) that I liked for its outrageous fluorescence. Not that anyone would opt to see it 'til I'm maybe twenty-eight. The whole virgin thing just gets on my nerves.

I had lunch with Lianne. Then we took a horse and buggy ride around Central Park.

"So what gives, Lianne? Why you been helpin' Mr. *SuperStar* so much?"

"Me?"

"Cut it out. I've been keepin' track, girlfriend. The flowers last year in the green room at the Soul Train Awards, the gifts that just *happen* to show up wherever I am in the country, and I just know you set that up with Sincere last night. That was so you. So spill the beans."

"Okay. Truth is that Douglass, aka Mr. *SuperStar*— as we like to call him—is in hot pursuit. We generally don't accommodate men who chase after our artists. But this guy? Not only do I *have* to deal with him for all of our artists and not only does he have the biggest cable audience in New York when it comes to black music, but he's more charming than a cool breeze on a ninety-eight-degree Bahama beach."

"YESSSS!" I gave Lianne a high five, yellin' like my favorite football team just scored.

"You betta go, girl."

"Oh, I'm tryin' to go. Don't worry! Don't you worry about dat, girl!" We both cracked up.

"What about Sincere?"

"He is over. Girl, if I told you what he did to me at Roscoe's in LA, girl, you would lose your freakin' *mind*!"

"No."

*"Yes!"*

"Can you give me a hint?"

"Nope. I ain't tryin' to go out like Tisha did Martin. He was wrong. I'm over it. Let his talent entertain the masses. And I'll do the same. Why should I go tryin' to sue this person, sue that person? Try to mess up his career? Me? Nope. Not I."

"Girl, you have come a very long way in such a short period of time. Wisdom. That's what you've got."

"Huh . . . sometimes I wonder."

"I envy you, Angel. Really."

"Just keep watchin' my back, Lianne. I'm takin' us to the top. The top of the world!" My hand shot up.

"Sounds like an idea for a song," she said.

"Somethin' to make you go *Hmmmm*." I smiled.

Lianne worked it out for me to have the limo for the rest of the day. I left Nitro and followed my heart all the way to New Rochelle, but we had to stop by a gas station just off the exit to find out where Main Street was. Mr. *SuperStar* was in for a big surprise. The limo pulled up to number 500 and double-parked beside a block full of parked cars. It *was* Saturday, so I figured others were shopping too. There were two glass doors leading into 500 Main Street. The first was open. The second was locked and there was a panel of buttons to buzz people into various businesses upstairs. By the looks of it, there weren't more than six offices. I recognized *SuperStar* immediately. There was a gold star stuck on the buzzer. As I was about to push it, a Spanish guy came down the steps and opened the door to leave.

"Excuse me? *SuperStar*?"

"Supa-star. Jess. Up-a-*stair* . . ."

*"Gracias,"* I said, using about the only Spanish I knew.

*"Sí, señora,"* he said and shot out the door.

I climbed the steps and thought of my first words in case I ran into Doug first. After the second flight, I peeked around and immediately knew I was in the right place. I smelled incense and I heard a subtle flow of jazz music. The office door was open. And before I stepped over the threshold I could see a couple of women at work.

"Ohmigosh!" exclaimed one girl. The other girl put a hand to her shoulder to calm her and walked up to greet me. The sunglasses are no help, I swear.

"Hi," the young woman said with her radiant smile. "Are you here for *SuperStar*?"

"Aah, sort of. I didn't make an appointment or . . ."

"Oh, *please*. Everybody knows *you*. Our boss just interviewed you last night, didn't he?"

I nodded.

"Please, come on in," the woman continued.

"Thank you." I was a little warmer now, a homey feeling I get when folks show love.

"I'm Jo-Jo," one girl said.

"Ohmigosh—uhm—" The excited girl squealed and I thought she was gonna bust.

"Hi, I'm a . . . oh . . . I . . . Doreen . . . Flourene . . . oh—ahh . . ." The girl stomped her feet and shook her arms in frustration.

"Please excuse her. This is Maureen . . . last I checked. Maureen. That *is* your name, isn't it?"

Jo-Jo looked at Maureen as a parent would, like she was thinking, *Get ahold of yourself, girl.*

"Excuse me. Hi. Uhm, excuse me. I've gotta go use the ladies' room." Maureen shook my hand and shuffled away as if I was the plague. I heard a scream a few seconds later. Jo-Jo and I smiled at each other.

Then she said, "I suppose she's a little excited. Would you care for something cold to drink? Or coffee?"

"No. I'm fine. Just ate not too long ago. Is—is Douglass in?" For the first time in a long time I was nervous. I wasn't even this nervous when I performed at awards shows.

"Yeah, he's somewhere in the building. I can have him paged. Wanna have a seat?" As she spoke I looked around the room. Different framed *Super-Star Magazine* covers filled an entire wall. There were all kinds of big names up there. Besides my cover there was Vanessa Williams. There was Tu-Pac, Snoop Dogg and Isaac Hayes, Toni Braxton and Da Brat, Janet Jackson and Rachelle Ferrell, Luther and Will Smith . . . It seemed endless. Then there were photos of Douglass with some other icons. Douglass and Michael Jackson, Douglass and

NUBIAN. No better reason for me to come back to my senses.

"Excuse me? Angel? Would you like me to show you around? He'd love it if I gave you the grand tour."

"Sure, why not?"

"Okay. Well, you're in our lobby and reception area now. Maureen is one of our loyal office workers. As you can see, she's also a music fanatic."

Jo-Jo was real nice, introducing me to everybody and showing me the television studio where post-production is done and the wing where writers, graphic artists, and editors published *SuperStar Magazine*. I was surprised to see that Douglass's business took up the entire second floor. I wondered when we'd run into him. Finally, Jo-Jo escorted me to the executive offices, where a woman had her back to me. She was on the phone, going over some photos on a big round table.

"Dee?" Jo-Jo interrupted.

She turned around and I immediately remembered her from my party the night before and the video rehearsal ages before that.

"Listen, I've got an important meeting right now. Can I call you back, sweetheart? Okay, good." She hung up and cast a smile my way. I felt accepted. "Hi, Angel. What a surprise!"

"Yes. That it is. Even a surprise for me—trust me." *Because, if my mother knew . . .*

"Hmmm. Well, I'm glad you came," Deidra said. "Should I announce you?"

"You mean he's here?" I pointed to the floor, meaning *this very office*.

"Right through those wooden doors."

There were double doors that could very well have been the entrance to a house in Beverly Hills. Opulence. A pair of golden *S*'s were at the center of each door.

"I'll show her in, Dee." Jo-Jo twitched her nose at Deidra and told me, "Hold on, Angelica."

The door was left cracked and I could her Douglass finishing a phone call. The mumbles. Then silence. Then a smack. I was sure it was skin that was slapped. Jo-Jo emerged from the doors. She was more meek now, but smiling in a proud way. I looked over at Deidra, but she lowered her eyes and turned away.

Her expression sort of said, *You didn't know, you betta ask somebody*.

"This way, Angelica," I heard Douglass say. There was that smile again. I caught a chill walking through the doors. I couldn't believe I had come this far.

"Close the door, darling."

"My, my, my, aren't *we* the lavish one."

"Only the best. I've worked hard for all I have, baby. Real hard. You like?"

I was fixed on the framed photo of Naomi. Perfect tits. "Herb Ritts?"

"Mmm-hmm. Naomi. That's me, Angel. Just *love* the female body. It truly is God's best work next to oxygen." Douglass came from behind his desk. "Listen, let me say something to you." He took my hand and led me to the corner of the office where a five-gallon fish tank was set in the wall. "I listened closely to your poem yesterday. And to say the least, it was deep. And incredible. And it made me real sorry I waited to see you all this time. But you must know that my business is important to me. If I didn't have a business, I'd never have met you. Right?"

I nodded.

"So how about you and me"—he placed my hands around his shoulders and his hands fell to my waist—"go back to where we left off. I think . . . there was . . . a kiss."

His voice was so soft and sexy. It made me weak. Next thing I know I was reliving the dreams I'd been having day and night. His long, sensual kiss was straight out of *The Young & the Restless*. The foundation seemed to be moving underneath me—or maybe my knees were buckling. It was so right—his tongue in my mouth, his hands smooth against my hips and back. If I were a lightbulb I'd be glowing at 150 watts. Blazing. But instead I felt like I was melting.

"You know I don't like to mix work and pleasure."

"Okay. So which one am I? Work or pleasure?"

"I'd like to find out. Can we get out of here?"

"Yeah, but can we kiss again? I sort of don't want that to end."

We went back to heaven on earth. Almost five or ten minutes of it, on his office couch, and almost on the floor.

"Ooops!" I covered my mouth, having noticed the bulge in his jeans.

"Yeah, that's what happens when girls like you get guys like me excited. It's natural. Call it a man thing." And look at *him*; all comfortable about it like he got a Boy Scout medal.

I was listening to him, but I was also thinking back to some of the stuff I've caught on cable TV and in one of those magazines in Lianne's office. The thoughts kinda turned things up a few levels.

"Give me a minute, babe. Be right back," he said.

While he stepped away I nosed around some more, imagining how things worked at *SuperStar* and what Doug does on a day-to-day basis in this boss environment. Fish. Birds chirpin' in another corner. All kinds of African masks on the walls. Plant life. I felt like I was in a jungle, except that there was jazz music instead of streams of running water.

"I swear you work in a freakin' rain forest with all of these animals and plants," I said when he came back.

"I guess. Feels more like paradise to me."

"Who is that we're listening to?" I asked.

"Oh, her? Rachelle. Rachelle Ferrell. She's a singer like you. Only, she has a more cultured voice."

"Cultured?"

"Experienced. All-knowing. Been there, done that. She's got more octaves than some people have teeth. I'm surprised you don't know her."

"Is she a jazz singer?"

"Not really. She can *do* jazz . . . scatting . . . a jazzy sound. Whatever. But I bet she could even sing country music if she wanted to. Problem is, she's not the commercial sound."

"And I am?" I figured. He shrugged in response, as if it was a shame. "I don't try to be commercial. The label pushes me that way."

"But baby, that's cool. It is. Different strokes for different folks, ya know. It's like teachers; they do one of the most important jobs on earth, yet they get the lowest salaries. Why? Who knows? But I think it's important that teachers get paid so little."

"Why?"

"'Cause then through the struggle we know that their concern is genuine. Their interest can't be purchased. It must be from the heart and their reward must be the good feelings they get out of contributing to society. Like Rachelle; she's like a teacher. Authentic talent that is to be studied and cherished—not squandered in top 40 airplay rotation. Her work is a proud work, for certain appreciative people."

"Wow. You sure know a lot. And it is depressing."

"Hey. Come 'ere. Come 'ere, boo-boo." He was pursing his lips with sympathy. "Look. You go on and sell your billion records. That's what you were put here for. To reach certain people with your particular message."

"But I wanna reach everybody."

"Ain't gonna happen. I don't care if you sang the slamminest rendition of the national anthem or the most riveting remake of 'Amazing Grace.' It ain't gonna happen. First off, you got people who don't like your color. You can never get past that. Then you got people that don't like black music, some don't even like music, whatever color you wanna call it."

"Damn, I never thought about it that way."

"It's like Bill Cosby once said: 'Your biggest mistake is trying to please everyone. You'll never be able to do it.'"

"You *do* know a lot."

"But you know what I really wanna know?"

"What?"

"You."

Douglass tickled me to death, his hands all over my body. We were on the floor again. And I loved it.

# Chapter 17
## DOUGLASS

**W**hen Angelica showed up at the office it caught me off guard. When I found out Jo-Jo brought her up to the office without calling me first, I smacked her on the ass. But she was enjoying that more and more over the past months. Still, I promised myself I'd be gettin' with Jo-Jo any day now. It was just the thing to do. And I noticed that, once the girls had some of "the Captain," they became more devotees than employees. After all, if another magazine or TV show offered them more money to leave me—and money was the only concern—I'd be running a ghost town. But *SuperStar* was different. There were those who just wanted to be around the fame, those who loved the idea of an all-black entertainment company, and of course, there were others who just wanted to be around me. I knew that if I decided to close shop and go deep-sea diving, I'd have a couple dozen bitches to go with me.

Like that.

I asked Jo-Jo one night, "When you started here as an intern, the first day, if I asked you to go to bed with me, what would your answer have been?"

"Are you kidding me? The night we were doing

the photos I was hoping you'd see through my dress. I wanted you that *night*."

So I thought about that. And I figure, maybe it's my aura. Like, I attract these women who want to give it all to me. And they feel so strong about it that they wouldn't have it any other way. Playboy? Player? Pimp? Captain Save-a-ho? No. I ain't none of them. I was born human—to want love, and to give love—just like everyone else. Now, what I've *become* is another story. The main thing is I keep it real.

I told Angelica to let the limo driver go and I took her to my place. I figured, *shit*, she came all the way to New Ro for *something*. So maybe I'll introduce her to "the Captain" too.

"Wow. The ceilings are like a mile high," she said.

"I need that. Leaves room for acrobatics, if you know what I mean." I don't think she knew what I meant, but I was sho-nuff 'bout to show her.

"So this is your crib, your big getaway from the business world?"

"Mmm-hmm. No business goin' on here. All pleasure."

"But you never answered my question from before. Which am I?" I felt her becoming adventurous again.

"Are you considered high maintenance?"

"Look at me. Tank top. Low-rider jeans and a pair of kicks. Do I *look* high maintenance?"

She was right. And I was ready to stop talkin' if she was. I already had her confidence with all the gerbil-snatch I was talkin' back in the office about teachers and pop versus jazz. Damn, she fell for that cock-and-bull so easy. Once she let me get my hands all over her, during the tickling, I knew from there that it was gonna be on and poppin'. And, as usual, there was nothing left to say. My calculations were simple. The girl was seventeen. So she couldn't have much experience. I was betting that she was still a virgin. So I'd have to take it slow with plenty of foreplay. We were back to the kissing, something I knew she enjoyed. Except there was something more serious about it this time, how we wouldn't be interrupted at all . . . how she was so far removed from her little celebrity world, with all of its protective fields. Angel's arms hung loosely at her sides as I worked my magic, taking her lips with my own gentle storm. She fed me back as best she could, but it seemed that she preferred to be taken than to take. So I took. And took more. Showing her all of my moves; how I concentrate on one lip, kissing it alone until the other one feels deprived. Then I switched up. Then there's that thing I do, slipping my tongue up between her teeth and gums, roaming the circumference of her mouth like a gumball that lost its way. Then I'd put my tongue full in her mouth, reaching halfway down her throat until she was caught between sucking and breathing. The whole time I'm giving her more and more of my saliva, the first of my bodily fluids I wanted to fill her with. She smelled *so* delicious, with the slightest amount of perfume on. I'm no professional, but I'd swear she had on Calvin. Still, it gave way to her natural scent, the aphrodisiac I preferred. A carnal pleasure.

In one move, as I nibbled on her bare collarbone, I reached past her lower back, grabbing her ass by the handfuls and snatched her up so that she was lifted in the air to hook her legs around my waist. She placed her arms around my neck. I walked that way, feeling my erection push against her butt, until we got over to my futon bed in the back of the loft. Then I eased down until she was on her back and I was hovering over her. Angel's eyes were glassy, searching for something more than passion.

I whispered, "Hold on," and left her lying there so I could turn on some music and close the curtains to the daylight. Luther. The Whispers. Barry White. Anita. Sadé. Marvin and the Stylistics. All sure shots. All of them pre-programmed. First up, the Isley Brothers. "Don't Say Goodnight." The words seemed so appropriate. I couldn't have planned it better myself.

*I wanna love you . . . yeah . . .*
*over and over again*
*I wanna see*
*see what your life can be*

I was catchin' chills myself, and damned if I didn't feel like this was *my* first time. I rolled down the bamboo blinds and the room went from loud light to a mellow sunset. From a distance I could see Angel's eyes, dilated and stuck in lust. Sure to let her in on my intentions, I stood over her now and pulled off my shirt. Between working out and visits to the dermatologists, I figure I'd spent maybe $2,000 to get my chest just right. So I wanted to show her that first and let her touch it.

I noticed a hint of fear in her face, her trembling lips. So I lowered to her again and planted assuring kisses about her forehead, cheeks, and earlobes to keep it fun. I worked my way below her collar—nibbling at her breasts through the tank top. I looked up at her, perched up on her elbows now, and immediately went down again with the idea that I'd soon be deep-sea diving. Her midsection was showing, something the world had already seen in her latest video. But they weren't kissing it, kissing her navel and hearing her squeal like I was.

While I kissed her, my hands caressed her sides until her yellow tank top was up over her bare beasts. And I kissed them. Angel was breathing hard. I could sense that she was silently wondering if I was pleased with her breasts. I showed more appreciation than she could stand—moaning like she was—as I encircled her nipples with my teeth, playing with them like the soft marbles they were. Cupping them, kneading them, loving them. She was on her back, squirming underneath me while I worked my way back to her lips. Kissing was something passé at this point. I'd reached unknown levels, ready to go to uncharted depths.

"Seems like you're ready. Girl, are you ready?" I sang to her, a bit of R. Kelly, and at the same time my forefinger played in and out of her mouth, smoothing her moist lips. I didn't want an answer. The situation didn't require one. My hand was unfastening our jeans now. My other held both of hers against the pillow behind her head. I couldn't help thinking, *If my friends could see me now*.

# Chapter 18
## ANGEL

I wanted to tell him to be easy, but it was hard to speak. I could hardly breathe, my heart was so busy in my chest. I was too overcome by the pleasure. There was the question of love, but I set that aside. I just assumed that this *was* love. In the purest sense. I was done playing hard to get. Tired of being Miss Goody Two-shoes for my mother and father. I was just so happy in the moment. Filled with good feelings and elations that were filling my whole body—like he was controlling my bloodstream, my senses.

There was one instance when I closed my eyes and through my lids, I saw a blinding light. And my body shook like the jolt you get from touching open electricity. But this was on purpose.

Douglass had me naked on his bed while he whispered in my ear. It was so crazy. My hands were held taut over my head. He talked me through every step, walked me through every engagement.

"This is just my pinkie," he said, already cupping his hand down there. Already becoming familiar. I felt it go in, like a tampon, only this was *alive.* He wiggled his pinkie in there and it made me squirm.

I just held him tighter, wanting him to keep talking. To make it all go right. After a time, he stopped and lifted himself up, looking down at me. I didn't even wanna look at how big he was, I just knew from touching it. He took my hands to have me hold it. It was beyond me how I'd take all of it. I chose not to think about it.

*Concentrate on the pleasure*, I kept telling myself.

I was so delirious that I didn't realize what Doug was doing. Sniffing. Kissing. Petting. Then he was licking me, holding my legs up, holding me open down there. My eyes closed again and I swear I was gonna black out from how crazy he was making me feel. His tongue was so smooth, making me quiver by the second. He teased me for a while. Then he just got all stupid down there, licking me like a dog. The sounds alone, all moist and gooey were driving me insane. I couldn't stop my cries. My screams. Plus he was ordering me now.

"Stay still, I said!" And I'd freeze my body just so—petrified at what was happening to me. "You like it?" he asked. I didn't answer. I swear, I couldn't. I was in some other world. Then he slapped my butt. It was my wake-up. I answered, *"Yes. Yes! I love it . . . Ooh, Dougie! I love you!"* I was hollering, with so many crazy colors passing before my eyes. I've heard labor pains before, like when Mother was having Tray. But this wasn't pain I was yelling about. It was a rainbow, a waterfall, and then an ocean. My body was acting on its own. Heaving. Squirming. Going through convulsions. Rising and falling with no rhythm whatsoever. Once I settled down, Doug was just laying by my side. Looking at me. Smiling.

"Did you like that?"

I closed my eyes and opened them, then said, "It was . . . it was the best I've ever felt."

"But we didn't even get started yet."

"Huh?"

"I'm serious. You see this? Go 'head, look at it."

I did. And yes, it was big. He was stroking it, too.

"This is Leroy. I'm gonna teach you how to take care of Leroy. You ready to learn?"

I was curious, but game. I would do anything Doug asked at this point.

I nodded.

"Okay, scoot down."

Doug grabbed a bunch of pillows and propped them behind his back. My head was down at his waist now. My legs folded underneath me.

"Now talk to Leroy. Go 'head. Talk to 'im. Tell him how much you wanna be his friend."

Doug had his hands clasped behind his head now. Lying back and very much in charge. I thought this was silly, but *whatever*. As good as he was making me feel, his wish was my sworn duty.

"Hi, Leroy. My name is Angelica. I'm a singer . . ." I giggled and Dougie smiled back at me. "And . . . uhm . . . I guess I'd like to know you better."

"Much better."

"Yes . . . *much* better." I turned to him and then back to Leroy.

"I don't think Leroy can hear you, baby. Move a little closer. Like you're whispering in his ear."

"Like this?"

"Mmmm-hmmm . . . I think Leroy would like a kiss. Give Leroy a kiss, Angel."

I kissed the tip. I swear it moved, and my eyes bugged out.

"You've got him excited. I think he likes you."

I kissed it some more. Held it with my hand until Doug told me to use both hands.

"Keep goin', baby."

I looked up to make eye contact with Doug every so often, to make sure I was doing it right. He nodded with slits for eyes, and I knew he was feeling good.

"Put it in your mouth, girl. G'won."

He smelled so fleshy and then it tasted the same. I took it little by little, curious as to how far he wanted me to go. As I worked my lips and mouth around him, I became amused at having such a large, throbbing muscle in my mouth. He was moaning now, I think. But when I looked up, he was smiling back at me. Confident and unafraid.

"Mmm-mmm-mmm," he uttered, showing his appreciation.

He did that a lot, as if he couldn't believe I was doing this, as if he couldn't believe I was here. I started to think the same thing, but that thought went away a long time ago. So did the one about the condom. He was holding a bunch of my hair in his hand now, controlling my head, urging me to move up and down on him. I didn't mind; if it made him happy, okay. He reached down with his other hand and toyed with my tits. Then he pulled me up so that I was on my knees with my mouth still down on him. He spanked me hard. I winced and responded with more friction, bobbing faster on Leroy. The idea of his penis having a name was funny.

"Come 'ere," Doug told me.

I did. He handled my body, turning me around again so that I was on my back with my legs spread apart. He went down there again and kissed me once, a quick one. Then came to talk in my ear again.

# Chapter 19
## DOUGLASS

**Y**ou like that?" I asked her, with my forefinger against her inner walls.

She nodded and moaned (with an umph) at the same time. I worked my middle finger in now. The both of them loosening her, preparing for me to go up in there. I took my wet hand up to see if there was any blood. None. Now I was sure I could go where my fingers had been. I pressed the same hand against the side of her head as I spoke to her.

"*Take me, daddy. Say it. Take me, daddy.*"

"*Uhmmm . . .*" She breathed. "Take me, daddy."

I was inside of her about an inch. She was whimpering, pushing my chest in resistance. I overpowered her and grabbed both hands to stretch them back over her head.

"I can't take you, baby, if you're pushing me away. Now keep your hands where I put 'em, and open your legs. Do it." I spoke through clenched teeth and handled her with firm holds. Tough love, I intended. "Now let daddy in, baby. Let it happen."

I fingered Angel's mouth and tongue, and once my two fingers were wet again, I inserted them, further lubricating the opening. Then I quickly replaced my fingers with that same inch of my dick.

"Can I hold you?" she asked, and then put her arms around me.

"Go ahead," I told her. "But let it happen, baby. Just let it happen." I was in her ear again, hands grabbing her braids in knots. I eased in and out of her. Slowly. Wanting more of her own natural lotions to accept me. She was breathing hyper now, all loud with her lips pressed to my ear, telling me no. All the while, I'm thinkin' *hell* no.

Then she's crying in pain. Bloody Mary. Grabbing all over my back. Then the nails—clawing me. Digging.

"No! Noooo! It *hurts*! Noooo!" The deep, carnal cries were deafening. I pressed my palm hard against her lips. The singer many millions would never know. The breathing stuttered. The sighs and whimpering rapid, like someone caught out in the bitter cold, naked and begging for mercy. All of the noises had me hard as a rock. Gettin' me off like I never imagined. Out of control, I busted off on Angel's pelvis. My body fell limp over hers, yet I could still feel my dick throbbing relentlessly, still spewing semen, wedged between her midsection and mine.

Awkward melancholy moments followed. Me feeling the turmoil inside, trying to show otherwise through my fake-ass smile. Trying to rationalize to find my own balance, my own peace of mind. Spent, but not satisfied, I made small talk, trying to smooth over the rough activities and the tough talk. Being all spent, with my sperm drying on our skin, I honestly didn't give a fuck anymore. No, there wasn't that normal completion. But as far as I was concerned, we did it. I got a little head, I got an inch or so—raw—up in her. *Fuck it.* If it was supposed to end here, then that's the way it'd have to be. Then she broke the silence.

"I'm sorry, Douglass. I'm so sorry. I wanted this to be right. For you to be happy . . ." I guess she saw through my phony smile. "Are you upset?" She was smoothing her hand on my chest, with pleading eyes and a timid tone.

"It's okay, really," I lied. "As long as I made *you* happy. As long as *you* were satisfied, baby." But inside I thought, *Oh, brother.*

"Can we try again? Is there like . . . something we could use to . . . help us?"

I thought, *Me? You need the help, girl!*

"*Some*thing?" I chuckled. "The only thing that will help us, baby, is time. Time fixes everything and I don't know if you have that for me."

"What are you talkin' about? How can you say that?" She spit the words in disgust. I was on a roll too.

"It's real, baby. Keep it *real.* You're about the busiest star, with all kinds of projects on your plate. That's success, baby. And there just ain't room for me. You barely have enough time for you. Be realistic; do you really think you can make it with me?"

Angel sat up, pointing and waving her finger. "See, that's one thing you need to learn about me. I'm *nobody's* puppet. You can call me a momma's girl if you want, think I'm Miss Sweet Cakes and all that. But until you've walked in my shoes, you can't call it . . ."

I was up on my elbows. Enlightened by Angel's new attitude. Then I said, "Where did all of this come from?" Trying to get her to spill some more emotion.

"Well, for your information, Mr. *SuperStar*, I've been thinkin' about this for a while. I'm my own woman. I plan to make my own decisions."

"Yeah? When? When hell freezes over? Do you think I'll hang around that long? I've got one life to live, baby. And a whole lot of other people depend on this one life. I can't stay in one place. Gotta move. Gotta grow."

"Okay, listen, Doug. I hear you. But I want you to hear me." Angel hugged up on me. We were nose to nose now as she continued. "I'm gonna be eighteen soon. On my own. My own place. I always told myself that whoever I gave this to would be the one. I told myself that I'd make it last forever, if I could."

As Angel looked into my eyes with her wishful thinking, all kinds of red flags went up. Commitment. Marriage. Soul mates. Forever. And I looked away, pretending to consider her words. This would take some work, I decided. And I also wondered if it was worth the work, until she spoke again.

"At age eighteen all the money that I've made is mine to use as I wish. If I wanted to give up my own profession and skydive in Australia for the rest of my life, I could do it. I'd have the money, and nobody but nobody can tell me what to do or who to do it with."

Why was my heart pounding like a drum? Why did she have to go and mention money? Is she out of her mind? Mention money, to me? I made a face like I hardly believed her. She went on.

"I'm tellin' you, Doug. Do you *hear* me? I've got millions in my account. Once I sign this Revelor deal, they're gonna give me even more. On top of that there's the new sitcom, the new album, all of it. I'm set for life." Angel nuzzled up to me. "*We* could be set for life."

"Yeah. Sounds good, doesn't it? The money. The freedom. But tell me, sweetheart, what's in it for me?"

She hesitated for a good ten seconds. "Me. All of me. I'm willing to lay it all on the table for you. I'll come to the table butt-ass naked if I have to."

"Butt-ass naked?" I kidded.

"That's what I said," she replied seriously.

"Yeah, you did say that, didn't you?" Silence. "But guess what, Angel?"

"Huh?"

"You're *already* butt-ass naked."

We laughed and fondled each other until I was erect again. And without me asking, Angel lowered her head and took me in her mouth again. I laid back feeling all-powerful, like the world was mine, along with everything and everybody in it. If I had my way, Angel, Angelica, Angelique—all of them were gonna become real good friends with Leroy.

# Chapter 20
## ANGEL

had it all figured out. It was ten months till my eighteenth birthday. That meant I'd be legal by the time we finished shooting the first season on *AN-GELIQUE*. I was ecstatic when the network picked up the show. From the door, they guaranteed two seasons. That meant a total of twenty-plus shows per year, for two years. I was also guaranteed $25,000 per show with an option to renegotiate after the second season.

Essentially, for my television work alone, I'd get a million dollars in two years' time. Douglass said I should've negotiated for royalties on future reruns because that's where the big money's at. But Mother handles that. For now.

Revelor contracted me as a spokesperson. I get cases and cases of free makeup and I keep the clothes I model in. The money is pretty good too. They also signed me on for two years at $250,000 a year. Why these guys are only lookin' two years down the line, I don't know. It's like everything's always contingent on everything else. It doesn't matter. The chips are stackin'. I had most of the makeup sent to New York for Doug's girls. I've gotten to like Deidra and Jo-Jo a lot. We've even gone out shopping on a couple of occasions, once when I came to New York, and once when I flew them out to LA. I swore Deidra had somethin' going on with Douglass, so when Jo-Jo stepped away to the restroom at the USA Mall, leaving the two of us, I asked her.

"So you like it at *SuperStar*?"

"It's great, Angel. Really great."

"And Douglass?"

"What? Do I like him?" I slanted my head and curled my lips at her. "I *do* like him. He's given me everything, Angel. I can't imagine life without him. The business is incredible, I'm satisfied, and I'll do anything for him. *Anything*. It's what he deserves. He's a leader."

"Oh."

"Angel?"

"Mmmm . . . ," I answered, looking at blurs of passersby.

"He loves you. And he wants you to be a part of the family. We're a team." Deidra had a warm hand on my shoulder, looking me dead in my eye. So sincere. I got ready to ask her specifics, like did she go to bed with him? But two little girls pushed up on us, shoving a pen and pad in my face.

"Ooh, Angel—*Angel*! Could you please sign my paper? *Pleeeeease?* Pretty *pleeease,* Angel!?" At the darnedest times. It never fails. Jo-Jo came back and helped to pull me away just when a group began to congregate. We escaped to another level in the mall.

"What about you, Jo-Jo? Has Douglass given you everything too? Does he love you, too?"

"Of course. It was hard for us to come see you, girl. And hard for him to let us go. But he loves you.

And he wanted us all to get a chance to be together. He wants a strong family. A team."

I thought about Deidra and Jo-Jo. I saw devotion from both of them in equal parts. For me to jump to conclusions would've been wrong. Of *course* he loves me. I invited the girls by the studio to sit in on a taping of *ANGELIQUE*. This was the date rape episode, where my friend goes out with this guy against my wishes, after I warned her that he was a womanizer, then after he rapes her, she has to swallow her pride and come back to me for help. These writers come up with the darnedest scripts. What happened to the comedy? Funny, I did kinda feel as if family was leaving when Jo-Jo and Deidra headed off to the airport. I promised to see them soon, and told them to kiss Douglass for me. I didn't mean it literally.

It's been quite a year for me. I'm looking at four more months of tapings; we finish in November. And I was offered my first movie part. It's small, but it's a start. Kara says she started that way too, but I think she was juicin' me up. Everybody knows she had a huge role in her first film out. Me? I get a handful of lines and ta-da—end of movie role.

Jingle and I are supposed to start working on the songs I wrote for my second album, but he just got a deal to do a soundtrack. So he's gonna push my project back, put me on two songs for the soundtrack, and fight for a big video budget. He says this would be a big boost 'cause the movie's got Miss Jada and Eddie in it. A guaranteed box-office draw. Plus the exposure, the production, the video and all the publicity wouldn't have to come out of my label

budget. The movie house would pick up the bill.
Lianne's cool with it too; she says it's *all* good for
the buildup to the sophomore album. Mother's been
asking me how I feel about things lately. I can't believe it. After all this time, my words finally hold
water. I get to add my two cents. But just wait 'til
November. Am I gonna drop a load on *her*.

**M**y album is still hanging in there on the Billboard pop chart. It went and fell off the R&B
charts. Everybody says the same thing: As long as
the TV show is on, your albums will always sell. So
I'm stressed at gettin' my project pushed back. I bet
Babyface wouldn't do me like that.

I finally got the Soul Train Award for best new
artist. Of course if you ask me, there wasn't much
competition, a couple of girl groups, a rapper, and
the Jamaican girl who's always pumpin' her coochie
in the videos. The Lady of Soul Awards wants me to
co-host with Brian McKnight next year and MTV
has been trying to sell Mother on a concept for an
amateur talent showcase. Such a blitz, all of this
celebrity work. The projects and events. Tomorrow
I'm heading down to Disney again. Tray's comin'
too. I told Mother that I wanted her to change my
security from Nitro to somebody else. He's spooky,
and I'm getting uncomfortable. Why can't he smile
sometimes? I don't know. I just don't need the nega-
tivity. He's so toxic. I'm expecting a royalty check
soon for my performance points on the first album.
Lianne tells me that if I wrote the hits I'd be getting
more money. Maybe next time. Why do I feel like
*she's* juicin' me? Like my check won't be what I

think it'll be. Mother and Father and I had a sit-down—they're becoming less frequent, thank God—where we talked about money. We're expecting, like, seventy-five cents from each album sold. So we got the calculator out and multiplied it by two million albums. I told 'em to multiply it by three million because the CD was still selling a few thousand a week if they considered international and domestic sales. But my parents—who I say just don't understand—want to keep the numbers "realistic." Ho-hum. So we figured the amount should be for at least a million and a half to two million. Then we had to subtract the advance of $200,000 in the beginning and another $250,000 after the third video came out. I remember that, too; Mother really had a time of it arguing with Mr. Nash. I had to nudge her while she was on the phone and tell her to chill. I thought the money wasn't all that important. But it is now. In the end, we expected a check for just over a million. My parents upped my weekly money to $750 from $500 and I even argued about that. Dag. Why can't it be a thousand a week? It is *my* money. But I didn't want to rock the boat. I think they were just tryin' to keep me in check. I swear, I'm gonna be Miss Rebellion in November. Earring in the nose, a few more in the ears, and I might get my nipple done. Douglass says he wants that for his next birthday gift. That and a tattoo over my coochie that says: For Dougie. He even mailed me a sample of it. It has a heart and an arrow with a bunch of leaves around it. I don't know about that, Doug. I just don't know. But why do I have the feeling I'm gonna do what he wants regardless?

# Chapter 21
## DOUGLASS

I've been maintaining communication with Angel in a few ways, besides hearing about her in the media. There's Lianne, who keeps me up-to-date on her movements, plus Deidra and Jo-Jo are still in direct contact with her. They tell me her every concern. It's like I have spies working for me since I even know all that woman-to-woman shit they talk about. I know exactly when her periods come, and the foods she likes. And I've been keeping notes. Only they're on my computer, not on my desk, like when Rain was around. That shit could get me in trouble all over again, to let these bitches know what's really on my mind. That reminded me; I had to have flowers and a card sent to Lianne. That woman should change her job title—I swear—to Pussy Deliverer.

"So what do I get for Christmas, daddy?"

"Humph . . . did I give it to you in the ass yet?"

"Ooooh . . . hearing that even *feels* painful." Jo-Jo lifted her head up from my chest, wincing at the thought, but half smiling, too.

"It ain't that bad, girl. You just gotta take it real . . . real . . . real slow. See? Watch me."

Deidra was going down on me, making me disappear in her mouth, while Jo-Jo and I watched. Lucky Leroy. I'm thinkin' about changing his name.

"So what are you sayin', Dee? Is your mouth supposed to represent your asshole? If it is, it's not tight enough!"

Jo-Jo and I hollered laughing. Deidra chuckled as best she could with me in her mouth. Then she bit me, but playful. She came up for air.

"Ouch! You bitch!" I cried loudly, but also playful.

"I swear, *your* mouth is like an asshole—with all that shit and vile coming out. Can we keep it sexy? Huh?" Deidra and her ethics.

"Go 'head, girl," I told her, and with my hand full of her braids, I pushed her back into her pleasuring me. She gave me the look and went on anyway.

"So?" Jo-Jo playing connect the dots, fiddling with my pectorals. "What are you gettin' me?"

"Well, you both have done incredible work for me. I feel like a king. So I'm givin' back. For one, we're going on a trip, all of us. I'm taking six interns with us too."

"Yeah?! Where?" Jo-Jo pounded on my chest.

"Easy. Easy, girl. It's a surprise. But that's not all. I'm thinking children."

"You mean, bringing kids *with* us?"

"Uh-uhh. I'm talking about you . . . having children."

"Whoa!" Deidra was up now. "Are you serious?"

"Wait a minute, I ain't tryin' to have no conference on the subject. Not now. Not while I'm getting my *dick* sucked."

"But listen, baby, this *is* a serious issue," Jo-Jo said, now with the speech. "When did you plan on discussing this with me?"

"With us?" added Deidra.

"O-ho-kay, this is some tag-team shit? While Leroy down there is deprived? Oh, *hell* no. I don't mind talkin' about it, but don't leave me out there like *this*." The girls looked at each other. Jo-Jo made a motion to Deidra, telling her she'd take her place, and Deidra moved up, hand on my bare chest. Kenny Lattimore was croonin' now through my speakers. Jo-Jo started with the cuddling, the kissing, and the lethal lips.

"So now, tell us, how did you plan on doing this? It's kind of major, baby. Really."

"Okay, listen. It's not really a Christmas present. I plan on getting jewelry and stuff. Clothes. Perfumes. You know, the stuff you guys like. The children, honestly? It's an idea I had a few days ago. I didn't really set up any kind of schedule. Although the trip would be real appropriate for it."

"So, you were gonna ask us—or tell us about it? I mean, having a baby?"

"Babies," Jo-Jo managed.

"Cut out the semantics, Deidra. Both of you have talked to me about having my next child, so don't even front."

Jo-Jo stopped to look at Deidra—a woman's scorn—then at me for tellin' her secrets.

"That's right. The shit is out in the open now. So cut the shit." I looked at Jo-Jo, nodding for her to continue. I was swollen now. Major blood rush. "Here's how I see it, boo. Life is really good right now. *Really* good. In a minute, it's gonna be so much better, so much more convenient. Money ain't a mutherfuckin' thang. You feel me? You both want children—so daddy's gonna give them to you. We're a *family*. A *team*. We work, live, fuck, suck, and we do it *together*. There ain't no mysteries here, girls. I'm about to put stones on your fingers, rocks around your necks, and my seeds in your bellies."

Deidra wiped a tear from her cheek as a crooked smile formed on her face, her nostrils flaring.

"Come on, baby. Smile for daddy. It's all gonna work out just fine." Jo-Jo was blowin' my mind down there.

"I know. I know it is." Deidra reached around to hug me, her bare breasts up in my chest. I kissed her forehead and urged her to join Jo-Jo. In time, both of them were slobbing and slurping religiously, forcing me to lay back, looking up at my giant screen and the silent images.

*Damn, that Heather Hunter gives good head.*

I was feeling like the lead actor with a supporting cast. Everybody in the company and in my personal life were making things so easy for me to grow and expand. The magazine was as thick as *Vogue* now, with advertisements from designers, makeup lines, nightclubs, restaurants, beauty salons, record labels, movie productions, even the Air Force and the Marines bought into year-long contracts. I had to laugh at that; the US government subsidizing my freak sessions.

We bought up the entire third floor of 500 Main Street. A few rooms were devoted to our live concert productions that we maintained on a monthly basis.

We've done the Beacon Theater, the Town Hall, and dozens of nightclubs. We wanted to bring the commerce home to the county where our office was located, but those racist motherfuckers up at the Westchester Center were fuckin' over the black promoters left and right while they laid out the red carpet for the white boys. To hell with that, I decided. I'll just keep my shit in the big city and ride with big-city aggression. *Damn* bringing it home. I'm tryin' to get this money.

Another two-thirds of the new floor was for my Black Model project. I set up the curriculum to bring in naked lambs who had a dream, and then to cultivate them to be better than video hos or strip-club bimbos. I figured as long as *I* stayed away from the girls, we'd have a good thing. The girls could slumber up for my TV shows and do fashion shows to include the designers who've been supporting the magazine. It's been hard, I have to admit, to stay away from those pretty-ass girls. I've seen Asians mixed with black, Puerto Rican mixed with Jamaican, and there's this Brazilian cutie who I wanted to push up on so damned bad! But like a twelve-step graduate, I'm taking it one day at a time. We pulled off four fashion shows already with money and sponsorships coming in by the pound. Plus, the TV show was leaving public access in January. It had gotten too commercial for community-based programming. So I shopped it to Fox. But they slept on the idea. Then I got a call from the parent company, an outfit up in Connecticut. They were looking to expand their black programming and recently acquired more than four hundred stations across the

country, boasting over sixty-five million subscribers.
I didn't jump at their offer immediately because I
was too busy getting drunk and celebrating. I don't
remember it all, but I think there was an extra sex partner that night. I think it was Sheena, but nobody's
saying. And then there was the hangover. When I
was sober, I went to Connecticut in front of a board
of directors at Lee Cable. I told 'em I was tired of
doing access TV and that it was time to grow. I told
'em flat-out that there are three other majors—
including MTV—who want my content. I tossed my
proposal on the conference table and told 'em, "Sink
or swim. I'll be at lunch. Please make up your mind
by the time I get back. Forty-five minutes, okay?"
Deidra followed me out of that room, by design. I
knew they'd be looking, gaping, open-mouthed at
my attitude, followed by her pretty round ass. I
came back a little more relaxed, my semen frustrations and ego deep in Deidra's digestive system, and
stood by for an answer.

"Douglass, sir, you've got a deal."

I'll never forget those words. They meant that the
*SuperStar* TV show and my other various productions were now subsidized to the tune of $1,200,000
a year for five years. I envisioned massive budgets,
elaborate expenditures, and loads of new profession-
als on staff. On the way back, Reno drove the new
Town Car. I knew that my actions were stepped up
and that my responsibilities were many. I also realized that the women around me were empowering
my drive, my aspirations, and my passions. I've
never done coke; I've always been too scared to mess
with drugs. Period. But if there was a high to com-

pare to this success, this empire, and these experiences I was indulging in, I'd have to say that there could be no such drug. Because I was feelin' it right about now. And I won't jinx myself, but if there was ever a downfall in my future, that might be just as great a tragedy.

# Chapter 22
## ANGEL

I wanted to make sure I had everyone's attention, so I chose Thanksgiving night to drop the bomb. I even had my clothes packed and stored at a room in the Four Seasons, just in case things got crazy at home; just in case Mom or Dad tried to get *real* with it and maybe tried to lock me in my room or chain me to a radiator. And I know that sounds a little extreme, but life was extreme these days. Just one look at the evening news and it was obvious that you never knew what to expect, even from your closest family members. So I had to have my Plan B in place, including the escape routes, the direction I'd be running, and the taxi cab phone number locked into a speed dial on my cell.

I took a deep breath and considered this to be Angelica's last stand. We were just digging into our servings of blueberry pie with a side of strawberry ice cream. My stomach was full of that good roast turkey that Mother makes every year, along with the candied yams, rice, stuffing, and the best baked potato in LA. We've been having more and more relatives over too, as if they were a measure of our success. I even adopted the quote: "Mo' money, mo' relatives." Fortunately, this year I influenced the family to keep the dinner simple. I told my parents that I'd appreciate a quiet family gathering. Just us.

"Excuse me, announcement time." I was tapping my spoon against a glass, making that distinctive clinking sound that always got folks' attention. Once the chatter settled I looked all my family in the eye; Tray was beside me, debating with Father about the football game today. I agreed with Tray, the Broncos rule. Mother had begun to clear the plates already and now she was lookin' at me all strange, thinkin' (I'm sure) that we never discussed any such announcement.

"Mother, please have a seat. This is very important."

Everyone got still as I cleared my throat.

"As you all know, January fifth will be my eighteenth birthday. I'll be of age, my own woman. Ready to take on the world . . ."

"Darling, does this have something to do with the money, or business? Because you know there's a time and place for that. Not during—"

"Mother! This is not business, this is *personal*. This is my *life*. Now, please. I'd appreciate it if I can be heard."

My father had a forkful of blueberry pie halfway in his mouth, frozen there in shock. I could almost see the words behind his eyes: *No she didn't just raise her voice at her mother.*

"As I was saying, my eighteenth birthday is a little more than a month away, and . . . I'll just cut to the chase. People, I'm moving out."

I had to swallow, not sure myself if I meant what I said. Mother looked at Father and Father looked to the ceiling, the pie having a hard time working its way down his throat.

"Baby, we can discuss that later. You're talking a month and a half away."

"No, Mother. I'm talking about *now*. I'm leaving today—*tonight*. I'm not waiting 'til January. I'm ready to leave."

"Where will you live? And with whom?"

"Where? With *whom*? Mother, I'm not a child anymore. First of all, I don't *need* any *"whom"* to live with me. I'm gonna get my *own* place. I can't say where right now, I'm still working things out. But I *can* tell you I'll be in touch to keep you informed of my progress."

"Keep us informed?"

I looked at my father. He was playing Ping-Pong with his eyeballs, switching between Mother and I, depending on who was speaking.

"Child, let me tell you something, I'm the one who keeps *you* informed. You don't inform me about *anything*. I'm your *mother*. We're your *parents*. While you're living under *our* roof and while you're *still* underage you will live by our rules. You will—"

"Patricia . . . Patricia!" my father cut in, and suddenly I could breathe a little easier. I didn't really want this debate with my mother in front of the others, but she was forcing my hand. And yet, I found it clever of me to even be prepared for this moment. I've dreamed about these possibilities over and over again. I had no idea she'd use that word—"*Child*"—to try to keep me in check, but most everything else she said was predicted. Thank God Father cut in.

"Honey, that's your daughter. But she's not a child anymore. She's a young woman."

Mother got into her feelings and left the table. I closed my eyes, not wanting to cry. But the tears started anyhow.

"Sweetheart, why don't you sit down? Take a load off." Dad was sweet about this, but I couldn't take the soft-talk right now. I was decided. It was such a relief to leave the house that day. I felt bad about the way it happened, but I felt happy too, liberated to be off on my own.

That night in the hotel was full of memories. I flipped through my photo albums, taking account of the good times. Our family picnics. Christmas. My graduation photos from dance class and acting school, the recitals I did and the performances at the family reunions. For a moment, looking at my baggage, my photo albums, and my three platinum plaques, I thought of how material and intangible life had become. A bunch of clothes and some plastic memories. I cried again. With my empty stomach in knots, and my cramps starting to kick in, my BlackBerry sounded off. I checked it hoping to see a New York area code. I missed Douglass and the girls. It was Jingle. Lianne's number was in there too. I must've slept through that call while I was lost in memories and tears.

"What's up, girl? You canceling for tomorrow? How come?

"What are you talkin' about, Jingle? I never canceled tomorrow. That's the Sprite Nite for B.E.T., right?"

"Whew! Man! Y'all had me goin' there for a while. I got a call from your people and they—"

"What call? What people?"

"Your booking agent got with me and told me all dates—concert and television—were canceled 'til further notice. I *knew* they had to be trippin'!"

"Jingle—where you at?"

"The Hit Factory. Downtown LA."

"I'll call you right back."

"Baby girl, I'll be waiting by the phone."

"Peace."

I hung up and immediately called Lianne at home. No answer. I paged her, 911, 911, 911. That meant to call me, even if she was on a plane, sittin' on the toilet, between movements. It meant call right now.

I paced the room, wondering about things. I had been saving money for this day. Less shopping got me $3,200 plus the $2,000 from inside my Elmo doll. And of course I had my American Express card. An abrasive symphony was playing in my head as I considered what the mixup was. There have been scheduling conflicts before. The promoter changing the date or the booking agency double-booking me—one agent unaware of another's commitment inside of the same agency. It's been easy to solve in the past. So I couldn't see why it would be a problem now. My stomach was talking to me. I dialed room service.

"I'd like to have dinner delivered to my room, please. Yes. Yes, this is room two-twelve. The manager? What for? You're kidding me!"

My AmEx was no good, they said. Couldn't tell me why. I paged Lianne again. Now the drums were beating in my head . . . a quick-time scat whippin' around with it. I sat on the bed, my legs crossed, hunched over to embrace my tummy. My foot shook uncontrollably like I was a drug fiend going through withdrawal.

The phone rang. The hotel manager called to say he needed to see me right away. He said no calls would be permitted to or from the room until I presented some form of payment. I wanted to yell at him *I'm Angel, you damn fool! Didn't you see my video? The Grammys? Don't you watch TV!?* But I kept whatever cool I had. I sat still to wait for Lianne's call for another few seconds until I remembered what the manager said. No incoming calls. Damn. I forgot my cell phone charger at my parents' house, so the hotel phone was all I had. I hurried downstairs to face a tall white man with a bow tie and tight lips.

"Look . . . my AmEx was working just fine yesterday. There must be some mistake."

"Ma'am, I'm sorry. You'll have to take that up with the credit card company. We have nothing to do with them."

"Well, I've got more than five thousand *in cash.* How much do you need for me to stay the night?"

"Ma'am, we're going to need a credit card regardless; it's a form of insurance in the event that there's any damage to the room. You know you rock stars . . ."

"DAMAGE!! ROCK STARS!!" I wanted to curse the guy out for gettin' on my last nerve. "I don't need your damn room anyway!"

I turned to go get my things, to get out of this snob-nosed place. But a big football-headed guy, with rocks for shoulders, wearing a pinstripe suit, was standing there like a wall. I almost walked right into him.

"I'm sorry, ma'am. You'll have to wait here in the lobby. The bell boy is retrieving your things."

Now my stomach *and* my head were hurting. And I swear steam was comin' out of my ears.

# Chapter 23
## DOUGLASS

**C**alm down! Calm down . . . okay, okay . . . I'm *not* yelling, just trying to get you to take control there. Now calm down . . . take a deep breath. Take another one. Let me hear it. Good. Now, take it from the top. And slow please. It's . . . it's three in the morning over here. You LA girls, sometimes I swear you get the extra three hours just to do your partying. What happened?"

I listened to Angel while I rose from the bed. I didn't want to wake Jo-Jo and Deidra, sleeping there, cuddling like they're attached in a dual fetal position. The Manhattan skyline was extra brilliant this evening, lights twinkling for as far as I could see. I had such a perfect view from our penthouse. Yet, in my own paradise—where it was all going my way, without conflicts or ills—I was suddenly interrupted by my worst enemy: DRAMA. I listened to Angel, her cussing her mother, telling me about money woes, credit cards stopped, something about the Four Seasons hotel manager kicking her out. DRAMA. It hadn't been this bad since Rain found that top ten list on my office desk once upon a time.

But while Angel was sharing her problems, why was I smiling?

"Okay, baby. Take it easy. Sounds like a management problem. But first thing, again, is for you to
take a deep breath. Relax. Where are you now?"

She told me about Jingle before and I've seen his
name in the trades. He did that hit soundtrack for
Eddie's last movie. An image came to mind of Eddie with buck teeth and bifocals, wearing checkered
pants and a disco shirt, trying to make it across that
freeway's rush-hour traffic.

"Yes. Yes, I'm listening to you, Angel." I stepped
away from the window and nudged Deidra. She
shrugged me off like a fly was irritating her. So I
shook her now. She was grumpy, but still lookin'
good, stretching in her birthday suit.

"It's Angel on the phone. Wake up; we need to
help her." I had my hand cupping the mouthpiece.

"What's wrong?" Deidra added on the end of a
yawn.

"Get up. I want you to talk to her. Keep her calm
and work it out so she's on the next flight out of LA."
Deidra reached for a crumpled, silk robe and took
the phone from me. Then she got into the whole
woman-to-woman conversation. Like Lianne, Deidra was also good at pussy delivery. Handle it, baby.

At 10 A.M. the day after Thanksgiving, Jo-Jo,
Deidra, and I stood at gate 13, waiting for flight
103 from LA to empty into the corridor. I'll admit to
some uncertainty tapping my nerves, but seeing the
anxiety in Deidra's face was a comfort. She had that
girl-thing goin' on with Angel, so I figured, *Just let
it ride, Doug. Let it ride.* If it ain't broke, don't try to
fix it—as my pop used to say.

The first passengers were lovebirds, strutting around the bend. Then a family of four, with the kids traipsing up the walkway. Angel was just behind them. Dark sunglasses, a trench coat, a baseball cap with her braids tied back and pulled through the cap's strap. Black, fuck-me boots reached up to the knees and she had a shoulder bag.

Deidra waved from the moment the star emerged. And she was still waving. Now Jo-Jo with the wave. *Okay*. I sucked my teeth, and joined in on the frivolity. Maybe it made Angel feel welcomed, because now she let a smile grow. Funny, it looked as if she had been in deep thought for the whole trip. And that she still had traces of a frown. But I ignored it, knowing there's hope in a smile. At the same time I was staring at Angel, Deidra ran up to hug her. Jo-Jo stayed with her arm around me, somehow proud of our new acquaintance and her latest decision.

Then the sunglasses came off, the shoulder bag dropped to the carpet, and Angel eased into a trot until she was close enough to jump up at me with the tightest embrace she could manage. We spun around, and I whispered in her ear, "Welcome home, baby. Welcome home." The spinning stopped. I felt her tears on my neck as she held on. Deidra and Jo-Jo stood nearby, trading slick smiles with me. My eyes saying *I told you so. Look at us now*.

Suddenly, I'm feeling a little like Charlie—with the Angels behind me, talkin' up a storm—as we headed for the parking lot. Once we were in the warmth of my Yukon, I felt more at ease. Eventually, I'd have to figure out our sleeping arrangements. We pulled around for the luggage, tipped the skycap real good, and sped off for Manhattan.

It was amusing to watch and listen to the girls talking among themselves. Almost as if I was in a ladies' locker room or standing behind a looking glass. Still, the action unfolded before me like an exclusive viewing of a John Singleton flick. And it was nothing but DRAMA.

"So that bitch actually played herself! She stopped my credit cards, my bank account is frozen, and she even had the nerve to cancel my concert bookings until further notice . . ."

Jo-Jo sat straddling a chair, chin on her clasped hands, quiet as a mouse. Deidra was helping Angel with her wardrobe, her suitcases all over the couches and the living room floor like a yard sale. I kept a straight face in the meantime. Not letting on that a smile was suppressed in my mouth. The girl was cursing! She was going the fuck off! I thought, *Is this the sweet momma's girl I once knew? Is this the Pollyanna who just went triple platinum, has her own television sitcom, and acts all cute in those Revelor commercials?* It was all stunning me.

"I'm supposed to be at the B.E.T. soundstage in Maryland for a four o'clock sound check and an eight o'clock show . . ." she went on. I looked at my watch. It was twelve noon. "And she called to cancel my performance. Told 'em I was sick. Fuck! *She's* the one who's *sick*."

I curled my finger at Jo-Jo and she hopped up from the chair. Now she was leaning over me for direction.

"Get Bob on the phone. Tell him the girl's over here with us and to expect her at the sound check as scheduled."

"Got it." Jo-Jo spun around to get to a phone.

"Oh, Jo-Jo?" She spun back, a little off balance. "When you finish the call, start putting together a press release. Make it politically correct, no wild off-the-hook statements. And explain that Angel is now under new management."

"Should I call it *Love* under New Management?"

"Very funny. Let me see the release before you send it off. We're gonna get the word to every Tom, Dick, and Harry in the business. We're gonna get our promotions staff together for a crash course in artist management. And by the time we're through, Angel's mom is gonna come to the bargaining table with her head between her ass cheeks."

"We still on for tonight? It's my night, ya know."

"I'm sure we can work somethin' out, Jo-Jo, even if it's gotta be in the back of the limo."

She smiled and raced to her duties.

Angel was still ranting. "I'm the one who got our family out of the apartments and into a house, new cars, all kinds of furnishings and clothes. Me. My *mother's* whole wardrobe is, like, top designers—because of me. But look at me! I'm pushin' jeans and kicks. You'd think that she'd learn some humility from her daughter. Then she wants to go and keep my weekly money at seven hundred and fifty dollars!?"

Deidra looked at me with that conspiratorial squint, as if to ask me if I was getting all of this. I gave a gradual nod. But the whole time Ms. Hollywood is ramblin'. Her accusations nonstop. *Her blood pressure must be on blast*, I marveled. I shook my head with a jerk and Deidra knew to scoot to another room. I let Angel talk herself numb, until she realized we were alone. Now she threw her arms up and they flopped to her sides. A gesture of hopelessness. She looked at me, my legs crossed, relaxed against the soft, white leather couch.

"So you're just gonna sit there? A big help *you* are."

"Hey. Don't get mad at me, Hollywood. I'm not the one with the issues. I just figured I'd let you get your shit off your chest and when you're done, I'll take over."

Angel took a deep, audible breath.

"Well, can you take over now? *Please?*"

I chuckled under my breath, knowing her frustration. And there was my curling forefinger again. Angel obeyed, slumping over onto the couch and against my chest. Immediately, I realized her fresh scent—the one I held onto at the airport—had given way to the odor of hard work and sweat. It was a reminder that, yes, the woman is human and while I'm thinking about it, her shit probably stinks too. The celebrity flame quickly evaporated, where I could see clearly that I had a new responsibility on my hands. A talented one, yes. But a responsibility nonetheless.

"Angel, I need *your* attention now. Look at me." She did. And her eyes were as glassy as when we were naked in my loft. "You're looking at your new manager. From now on, your career is in my hands. You have absolutely no worries about a place to live, about credit cards, hotel managers, *or* your mother.

You have no financial concerns whatsoever. *Got that?*"

She nodded. Those sad, surrendering eyes were so sexy.

"How we work here is simple. Everything that we do, all the money we make—*any of us*—no matter what or how we make it, goes into the pot. The pot in turn pays our bills, keeps us in the highest standards of living, and ultimately we eat. We eat *real* good. And do you know who controls the pot?" Angel was listening closely and her eyes connected to my own. Not a blink.

"You?"

"Correct. Me. And *why* am I in control? Because you trust me, don't you."

It wasn't a question. But Angel nodded. With that, more than ever before, I was empowered and enthroned. It was all a matter of time now. The next month and a half was important. She'd be eighteen and of age on January 5. There were legal concerns to pan out and a campaign to begin.

# Chapter 24
## ANGEL

Arriving at Douglass's penthouse was something like entering Shangri-La—just like the movie. Everything seemed perfect. The first thing I noticed was the sunken living room with the white marble floor. There was a white grand piano up near the glass patio doors, and only a few large pieces of furniture like couches, coffee tables, and a fully loaded entertainment center. There was a pool table too with marble balls. Every corner of the penthouse had huge, leafy tropical trees that provided the color in the place. All the wall hangings were exotic photos of beautiful women in seductive poses. Doug showed me the rest of the place—the bathrooms with the Jacuzzis, the master bedroom, and the kitchen. We didn't go out on the patio—too cold— but there was a Jacuzzi out there, too. All I could say the entire time was *wow*. I was intoxicated by all of the luxury. He, or *they*, were living so good. When I asked him where Deidra and Jo-Jo stayed, he responded with, "I've got three bedrooms in here, babe. Don't sweat it. Room for everyone."

"Where do I sleep?" I asked.

He lifted me off my feet and said, "Right here in my arms, baby. Now ask me about your pillow." He smiled that infectious smile, and I was weak again—forgetting all of my immediate concerns.

I was on time for the B.E.T. event. Folks looked at me real strange that day, like I had a "Smack me!" sign flashing on my forehead. But all in all, I enjoyed myself. Jingle handled my music, the live band, and the deejay, while Shatima was the lead dancer in a group of eight. We did a medley of four selections from my album, which I swore would be my last live TV performance until my new project came out.

Jingle says we're shooting for a second quarter release, despite when everybody else *thinks* my music should be released. He made good sense sometimes. Because if Whitney comes out in the first quarter, everybody's gonna be judging us like we're competing. And I definitely *don't* want that. I'm also writing most of the album. *Mo' money!*

**V**anessa Williams sang at the B.E.T. event. So did Angela Windbush, Stephanie Mills, and Chaka Khan. For the life of me, I can't figure out how I was grouped with these legends. But I was determined to hold my own. The event was billed as B.E.T.'s first annual *Songbirds* show. The answer to VH-1's *Divas.* I wasn't all stressed-out like I am for regular live concerts because this was for TV. Even if there was only half the audience, it would be okay. Besides, on recorded shows they always showed only the best audience shots anyway. If I messed up somehow, and it was so bad that I might be embarrassed, the producers would shoot the number again. That left me with a sense of comfort. And I did my thing with no problem. Folks loved it, too. The reviews were mostly positive. Not to mention that Lianne received a call from Mariah and got me on a conference call using the triple 911. Mariah told me I *went to church* on the *Songbird* show. She said she caught chills on my song "Love Is Our Dream," and she asked me to repeat the second verse of the song, so I sang it right on the phone:

*There's a reason for everything*
*Some may be poor and some are kings*
*But we are all human beings*
*With a lot of hope and fantasies*

*We may agree to disagree*
*We may live far beyond our means*
*But you and I both have our dream*
*Our dream is a love that sets us free*

The song is a ballad, a torch song that Jingle says could win me my first Grammy. The first album earned Grammy nominations. But this time I wanted the Grammy itself. Mariah told me she'd push for votes. I cried when we hung up.

"That's positive," Douglass told me. "You need to continue to network with other performers. We call it politickin'. Remember that you are a walking, talking institution. Positive relationships are your bread and butter."

That man is smart.

From the day I came to New York, I've been sleeping in Doug's bed. But because of my traveling,

we rarely get time "to play," as he calls it. The first
night we *did* get to play, we did a lot of touching and
holding, and our lips were everywhere. Mine were
mostly used to get to know Leroy better. However, it
didn't get any further than that. We both fell asleep.
He's had me working really hard, and he's always
explaining to me how hard work reaps rewards, as
long as I keep a healthy diet and a good exercise
schedule. The four of us have been doing virtually
everything together. For starters, we eat together.
He's got two cooks—one in the day, one at night. I
like the salmon and lobster dishes. Deidra hogs all
of the crab legs, suckin' on them all noisy 'n' shit.
You'd swear she's been with Leroy as good as she
sounds. Doug says we're all going away during
Christmas. Says he has a big gift for each of us. I
can't *wait*. We've already been to the Poconos. I
went skiing for the first time. Almost busted my ass.
We stayed in a lodge with adjoining rooms. Finally
time to get our groove on. I wanted him more than
he could ever know. At about midnight, I thought I
was hearing things in the next room where Jo-Jo and
Deidra were sleeping. Only it didn't sound like they
were sleeping. It sounded like . . . well . . . at least
they could've told me. I would've understood.
      Meanwhile, Douglass was teaching me some
things. Taught me how to handle Leroy with two
hands, how to massage him. He said he liked to hear
the slurping noises. After a long time he flipped me
over and showed me doggie style. But this would
still count as my first time, because that experience,
back at his loft in New Rochelle, I couldn't really
take it all. I was yelling for sweet Jesus the whole

time. But Douglass said he knew "where we were at," and that he'd handle it accordingly. I was on my hands and knees for a moment, all in the mood and ready to bite my lip, when I felt something slimy being spread on my coochie. When I turned to look back he forced my head down into the pillow, letting me up just enough so that I could breathe. That's when I felt him going in. Oh, God! I felt that pain again. I tried to yell but the pillow muffled me. My arms were flailing, but now he was holding them, too. Over my head. I felt like a Raggedy Ann doll the way Doug was manipulating my body like that. It was crazy too, because all the while I think I'm making noise, the noise in the next room is getting loud too. Then I felt more pain. I couldn't tell if he was all the way in, I just know it hurt like hell. Fuck! I never imagined that I'd hate sex so much. The stinging was like touching a hot stove without taking your hand away. More time passed, with him still hunched over my back, and his weight pumping me from behind until I was numb down there. The pain was still there somewhere, but so far gone that I stopped resisting. I just lay there on my tummy while he went on and on and on and on. He was saying things, baby this and baby that. But I wasn't listening. I was delirious . . . wondering how I ever imagined there'd be pleasure in this. Or love. Still, I heard laughter next door. Giggling.

# Chapter 25
## DOUGLASS

I stood naked in the bathroom mirror for a long enough time to watch myself wither. I'd been stiff ever since my orgasm. Ever since Angel fell asleep. My stomach was a little queasy—not happy about what I had to do. But, shit, that's tough love. If I didn't open her up, we would've been dilly-dallying for the next who knows how long, and I'd either have to do it then, or someone else would. I did use butter. I wasn't *that* hard on her, either. The screaming is natural, like a loud, day-long rainstorm. But flowers always grow and the earth always appreciates the gesture. So that's me, fertilizing her earth. Growing flowers.

"You guys were kinda loud in there. She all right?"

"She will be." I was speaking to Jo-Jo's reflection, standing behind my own. "I know she won't be able to walk in the morning. But the worst of it is over."

"Don't I know it? I remember my first time. I almost climbed the walls."

"Wish I coulda been there."

"No you don't, either. Almonte still has scars on his back."

"How do you know?" I turned to see her face-to-face.

"Trust me, I just know. Girls talk."

"Uh-hmmm. I pulled out. My wasted jewels are dryin' up on her ass right now."

"That *is* a waste." Jo-Jo was close to me now. "So are *you* all right?"

"Just a little crazy, that's all. Doin' virgins has never been my favorite."

"But you like 'em young, Doug, so how else would they be? There's no experience like experience."

"Mmmm-mmm-mmm." Jo-Jo put her arms around me, looking down. Holding me now.

"It's been a while since I've had this to myself, daddy." There I was shaking my head with an exhausted expression.

"Yeah," I said, not paying much attention to the implications behind her words. I looked down again. Then I said, "You all have to work with her now, ya know?"

"Hmmm?"

"I mean, she's almost a patient now. Bedridden, I'm sure, for at least two days."

"I can call the office. Have Maureen and Sheena look after things. Plus I'll tell the reservation desk we're stayin' awhile."

"Good idea."

"She's a special project, you know. Gotta be treated with TLC."

"*That* I don't have patience for. You know me . . ."

"Yeah, *too* well. You're an in-and-out kinda guy." Jo-Jo threw me her quick wit and seductive eyes.

Then she looked down at me again. Even I couldn't believe an erection was growing.

"You mind? I didn't have desert."

"Didn't you guys have enough of each other last night? *Damn*. Angel must be dead in there after you and your lethal lips."

"Mmmm . . ."

Jo-Jo was finished talking, already on her knees. I stood there looking in the mirror again. My hands combing through her wavy hair, and then holding on just to keep my balance. Because Jo-Jo always aimed to please, and because I was spent two times over, I was forced to ask for mercy.

"Just go easy, Jo-Jo. Easy."

It was Thursday, the eve of Christmas Eve. Most of the entertainment industry takes off from work early on these days, the "eves" that preceded the actual holidays. But the few who stay at work are diligent, devoted marketers, or even independent businesses, which are relentless in their efforts. The *SuperStar* staff was busy with the January/February issue, distributions, assuring that the magazine was delivered to the various merchants on time, and enough so that they'd last through (at least) late January.

The March issue would hit the streets in February. April in March, and so on. Regardless of how early the publication was delivered to clubs, salons, and various other businesses in the Tri-State area, we could never stack enough, both because they were free and because they were in heavy demand. The new covers, the front and back of the magazine, had exclusive photos of Mary J. Blige on one side and Babyface on the other. There were exclusive interviews inside.

The Black Model project was also in full swing, with lots of girls rehearsing up on the third floor, preparing for the big fashion segment of our Holiday Extravaganza on the forthcoming Saturday evening. Anita Baker was set to be our headliner, with Will Downing booked as the opening act. We expected an adult audience, one which would also appreciate fashion. So I figured, why not? Put the girls to work, because all they've been doing is looking pretty for our video productions and hosting many of our promotional parties. The swimsuit video was due out in March, so a fashion show would be good exposure and something different to see between sets—during intermission.

Meanwhile, our Internet venture was up and running, ready for a live webcast of the event, and Darryl had an eight-camera crew set to shoot the production for the LEE CABLE syndication. In total, we were looking to hit 100 million or more impressions of *SuperStar* products and content through the New Year. And it would all start with this very big and very important week ahead.

"Doug, Lianne from Artistic on your private line."

"Can you take it, Dee?"

"She's hysterical, boss. It's about Angel."

"Put her through." I closed my Internet connection and ended my phone call with Russell. "What's up, Lianne?"

"What's *up*? I'll tell you what's up! I've got a lawsuit on my desk, Doug! Nash has a copy . . . his name is on it. And the president of the parent company gave him a call yesterday. Douglass! They're all pointing at *me*! ME! I'm a damned publicist, Douglass. I'm not a business owner or an artist or an executive. I'm a damned peon! I could lose my job *just like that*! Can you *hear* me?"

Yes, she *was* hysterical.

"Lianne. You need to calm down. I got a copy of the lawsuit the other day. After all, my name and company are on it too. Don't you think I saw your name?"

"You *had* to."

"That's right. Now, how long have you and I been working together? How long as associates?"

"I dunno, maybe seven or eight years."

"Yes. That would be about right. But guess what? I was dealing with the publicist before you, too. Plus I work with maybe fifty others in the music industry. That doesn't include the movie production companies and if you count the video and television industry, we're reaching close to one hundred million people in and outside of the United States."

She blurted, "Can you tell me what the FUCK that has to do with the price of peanut butter? *Or* my job?"

"Hey, watch your mouth, Lianne. Watch your *mouth*."

Silence.

I was sipping a ginger ale.

"Doug? Doug? Are you there?"

"Mmm-hmmm."

"How come you're not saying anything?"

"I'm waiting."

"For what?"

"An apology." I could hear Lianne blow out steam.

"Douglass, I'm sorry. I must've lost my head."

"Well, let me help you get it back. My point was this, Lianne: Lawsuit schmaw-suit. This is a bunch o' shit. It means *nothing*. The girl's mother is bluffin'. Going on a hunch. No credibility to this document."

"Douglass, Douglass, Douglass. You don't see how serious this *is*. They're accusing you of kidnapping, embezzlement . . . And Doug? Did you see the words *child molestation*? Do those words *mean* anything to you? You could be shut down."

"Thanks for your concern, Lianne. But I'm not impressed. Neither are my lawyers. They laughed when they got this."

"So why am I getting all the heat if this is so unimportant?"

"You said it yourself, Lianne. You're a peon. A scapegoat. Even after eight years with Artistic." She sighed over the line. "How old are you, Lianne?"

"Twenty-six. Well, I will be in January the eighteenth—if I can stay out of jail that long."

I ignored her tirade and said, "Capricorn, huh?"

"Mmm-hmm," she muttered in a most somber tone.

"Do you want out of these problems? You want to breathe a little easier?"

"Oh-hhh-*hooo* . . . that would feel *so* good right now."

I looked at the wall clock across the room. It was noon.

"Tell you what. At one o'clock, be outside on the Fifty-second Street side of the Warner building."

"Huh?"

"Lianne. For the past eight years you've been doing as I ask. Keep it up. Please. One o'clock. And look for a jet-black Town Car. The plates have an *S* on them." I hung up and paged Reno to my office.

At 2:30 Lianne showed up and Jo-Jo escorted her into my office. She didn't look the same as the last time I saw her, at the B.E.T. event. She still had the fashion-model facial features, but her face was paler and her hair was out of whack—dirty blond, unstyled. She wore a skirt and pumps, the usual tight-ass corporate attire. Maybe she had contacts on, 'cause her glasses weren't on as they usually were.

"What happened to your glasses?" I asked her.

"I had that eye laser work done. Fourteen hundred per eye."

"Oh, you must be gettin' paid nicely over there. Three thousand dollars' worth of work on your eyes?"

"It was worth it. I don't need glasses to see anymore. When I'm reading it's a different story."

I kissed her cheek and held her hand to lead her to the couch under my giant fish tank. She gazed around.

"So tell me . . . what else did you buy? Liposuction? Breast augmentation? Your nose looks the same."

She smiled, and I knew the ice was broken. I already knew she was a genuine soldier, there as my resource for eight years. I just wanted her to deny it.

"Sorry, Douglass . . ." She straightened up—maybe to let me see it all. "This is every bit of me. The real McCoy."

I nodded in agreement. As if I was pleased or proud.

"So tell me, what brings you here?"

"Douglass!" She lit up.

"Okay, okay. Easy. Lighten up." I gripped her shoulder with my hand. Enough to make an impression in the fabric.

"I brought you here to make a proposition. A big one." I picked up my remote to lower the volume on my sound system. Lianne sat with her chin in her palm, and her elbow perched on her crossed legs. I had her total attention.

"Now, before you make a decision, I have some things I want to show you. But up front I'll say that I appreciate your work. You're very honorable and devoted to your job. However . . ." I took her free hand in mine and patted it. "You're not being rewarded for your full value. I think your work in publicity ought to be appreciated to the tune of one thousand a week, plus use of the company car, benefits, and associated perks. I believe you deserve commissions for all your work that is beyond the call of duty. I'm talking residual income. Do I think Angel's CD would've gone triple platinum without your hard work? No. Would she have the exposure, the incredible press, and the host spot for the Lady of Soul Awards? No. I think not. I believe your work and your labor is the reason she made it big. Everybody's been saying how unprecedented the massive support was. How instrumental your part was in the project. So the fat and skinny is that you're the reason, girl. It's you. Millions of people have talent out there. Many, many black girls. Some have even more talent than Angel has. But Angel had *you*. And I believe you have that magic to turn nothing into something. We need that magic at *SuperStar*. Please, follow me."

As I expected, Lianne looked at me like I had just asked her to marry me. Mouth half open, eyes pinned on my lips, pulling words out of my mouth faster than they came themselves. By the second, I was changing any idea that she had about priorities—which ones she had and what they meant to her.

With Deidra and Jo-Jo as tour guides, Lianne was navigated through the guts of the company. I followed behind a few paces, hands behind my back, eyes pursuing my interests—both still life and in motion—while in my own conversation with Phil, who was meandering alongside me.

"It's getting pretty big, Phil. The money. The women. My lifestyle is beginning to imitate my wildest dreams."

"So what do you need from me, D? Talk to me in English. I'm all ears."

"You know as well as I do that there are the well-wishers and there are the ill-wishers. That and the fact that things happen in cycles. We never know how or when, but shit tends to hit the fan. Know what I mean?"

"Maybe. You expecting trouble? Feeling threatened?"

"Phil, I'm a black man who built a multimillion-dollar business within the space of three years. I've done it mostly off of hard work, but people are easily gonna think it's tits and ass that made this happen."

"Well, that's all *I* see, D. And plenty of it."

"But that's just it. We're sleepin' if that's all we're concentrating on. Blind and stupid. The world doesn't wanna see a black man rise like this. It's too obnoxious. Too much against the template that's runnin' things. The bottom line is I need protection. Not the drunken auxiliary cop I was forced to hire back in Mt. Vernon, or the lugheads, the big dumb blocks that we've been paying to be security at the concerts and parties. Phil, we need presidential force. Nothing less. Intelligence, muscle, stealth."

"Maybe you need an army?" He was kidding.

"Maybe we do." I wasn't.

# Chapter 26
## ANGEL

"You remember that sports agent who left his partner and took his clients with him?"

"Yeah." I could hardly hear Lianne from my distance.

"And that Eisner guy who left CAA, he took some of the biggest actors in the world with him."

Silence. Lianne nodded.

"Well, it would be almost the same thing with you, Lianne. All of your contacts, your resources, and your relationships. Your computer's hard drive for God's sake, all of it. You bring it with you and I'll set you up at *SuperStar*. A bigger salary. A commission for Angel's growth. A bonus for signing, and all the fringe benefits."

"I won't have to get your name tattooed on my privates?" Lianne looked over at me and I wanted to *kill* her. That was supposed to be our little secret. I love her, but I swear she's a bitch.

"Oh, you heard about that, huh? Listen, I don't force anybody to do anything. And besides, the only people who get the tattoo are those who love me . . ." Then he looked at me. "And those whom I love." He blew a kiss. I love that man.

"Well, I'll tell you right now, Douglass. If—and that's a *big* if—I should decide to come aboard, it will be strictly business. Clear?"

"Oh, sure. I wouldn't want it any other way."

Doug looked over at me again, wondering, I'm sure, just how much I told Lianne. Ooooh, I wanted to kill her.

"All right then. Can I sleep on it?"

"Sure you can." Doug looked serious now. Not a hint of playfulness about him. "But if you leave here today without giving me a yes or no, the deal's off." Doug got up, coming over to me now.

"But wait. I thought—"

"You thought wrong, Lianne. You see this girl here . . . this woman?" Doug gestured for me to rise up. And I did. "She doesn't have time to think over her life. Her life is *now*. If she has to stop to think about whether she wants to take a breath or not, she'll die. In other words, baby, this is a life or death proposal. Now don't play games with me. You're in or you're out. Sink or swim."

I took a deep breath. I couldn't believe he laid Lianne out like that. I just stood there, my arm around my man's waist, lookin' at Lianne like, *Whatchu gonna do, girl*? In a frustrated sigh full of angst, as if she was concerned that she had no other choices, Lianne exhaled her answer. I jumped up and down, all silly, and ran over to Lianne to hug her.

"Aren't you excited, girl?"

"I . . . uh . . . yeah! I just—well, it's a snap deci-sion, ya know. My life has never been that way.

Hasty moves. The impulsive ways . . ." Doug went over to his desk, picked up his cell phone, and headed out to where Deidra was working.

He stopped to say, "Life is about opportunities, Lianne. Opportunities always come with risks. If you don't take opportunities, you'll never grow. You two chitchat. I'm gonna be down in the car. Next stop, Manhattan. Hurry up." Doug closed the doors and I just about squealed with joy. Then I remembered Lianne's big mouth.

"I can't believe that shit you just said, Lee! That was our *secret*."

"I didn't get specific, Angel. Maybe a hint . . ."

"A hint? You opened your mouth like a fuckin' book, Lianne. Shit!"

"Angel, what's gotten into you? You've changed so much in the last few months. You're cursin' now like a yuck mouth, your cleavage is out to here, you've taken your pretty braids out, and what's with the earrings in your navel and your nose?"

"Hey, this is me. My man likes it, so it's all good. He didn't *tell* me to get all this. It's just the real me. When I get onstage, I'll be the same ol' Angel. I'll take the rings out. Play the part."

"Girl, I told you before. An artist like you is *always* onstage, whether you're in the mall or at the White House."

"*Fuck* the White House. They ain't never done nothin' for me."

"Oh, see that? Yuck mouth."

"I am a star, see me SHINE!" I stood up and did a spin. My arms extended like I was reaching for the ceiling. "Let's go, my *man* is waiting for us," I was proud to say.

**D**ouglass dropped Lianne off at her place in Queens and we flew across the expressway to Manhattan.

"What happened to Reno?" I asked, with my head against Doug's shoulder.

"He's more of an errand boy, baby. Phil here, he's our new driver. He goes where we go, if you know what I mean."

I nuzzled up on Doug, feelin' all secure and protected.

"At least he's not like that Nitro, the guy my mother hired. He was such an ass. Wouldn't even let my fans come up to me. Actually knocked one to the ground too, saying he could've attacked me. Crazy."

"I remember him," said Deidra. "From the birthday bash. I wanted to smack the shit out of his pretty ass." I gave Dee a high five.

Doug said, "Those days are over, baby," with his hand all up on her thigh. I didn't mind. We were all family.

**T**he holiday extravaganza was here, and I couldn't wait. I had to take the express flight to Atlanta where I taped my duet with Gladys Knight for her holiday special. We sang "Santa Claus is Coming to Town" with a bunch of children around. Jo-Jo came with me, and Doug's bodyguard, Phil, escorted us the whole way on and off the plane, in and out of limos, and back to Manhattan. I had just enough time to shower and change.

There was this dope navy panne velour top and
pant set I wore. It was sprinkled with starbursts of
silver. Douglass bought it for me when we went up
to Caribana, the Canadian festival. The set was so
soft and sexy—somewhere between dressy and casual. There was a matching kettle-brim hat with
wool felt strips, horse hair, and silver metallic em-
broidery, all finished up in a classic bow. When I put
it on I looked like I was a whole other person, gift
wrapped for my man and his big event.

This was the first Christmas holiday that I wasn't
home with the family. But I hardly missed it on account of my whole busy agenda—feeding the homeless at a local soup kitchen in New Rochelle, giving
out presents at the Northside Children's Hospital,
and singing at the Mother Hale House in Harlem. I
swear I cried like a baby at each event, seeing the
sick children, the homeless folks, and the AIDS pa-
tients. It was all so humbling. It showed me what
life's difficult side was like and made me wanna
work harder. Doug always told me about hard work.
Smarty-pants is always right.

I called Jingle and wished him happy holidays. He
told me he'd be delivering a gift to Tray for me: a lap-
top computer. My parents would have to bite the bullet this year—as stupid as Moms was acting with the
money, the lawsuit and all. I didn't care. Come January 5, I would be LEGAL, BABY! It got so busy, and
Douglass and friends made me feel so comfortable
and secure, that I didn't even *care* about the money
in the bank. If I got it, fine. If not . . . *fuck it*.

The only other gift I bought was a diamond ankle
bracelet for Jo-Jo. It matched the one Sincere gave

me, which was my gift to Deidra. Been looking to get rid of that thing for a while now. The one thing I couldn't get rid of was the tattoo with Sincere's name down there near my cat. But I had this amazing tattoo artist from the Village make this crazy design where he changed it to say Doug's name with a heart, an arrow, and a bunch of leaves around it. You can't even tell Sincere's name was there.

I remember showing the new tattoo to Doug on Christmas Eve while we were lying by his fireplace. I made a ceremony of it. And then he made a ceremony out of me. Showed me a few new positions, like the one with my ankles touching my ears. I never thought I was so flexible, but I'm a believer now.

When the girls and I showed up at the big bash on Christmas night, I thought I was dreaming. Like, this was Hollywood—New York City style. There were swinging searchlights skating across the black sky, crossing the moon like giant Ping-Pong balls without rest. The press came out en masse. There were cars, cars, and more cars. Lexus. Mercedes. Hummers. Limos. Four thousand guests crowding through the barricades and the front entrance in an orderly fashion. Intense. Of course Phil escorted us right through the puzzle of people. MSG was sold out, with the show soon to start. We were ushered through the lobby—its opulence enhanced by balloons, flowers, and confetti—then up some stairs where our box seats were reserved. I suppose Doug had made power moves all over the place because my album was playing as background music in the auditorium while the audience came to wait for the opening act.

Finally Doug slid in the booth behind us, all done up in a tux, Kinte-colored bow tie and cummerbund and black loafers. Leave it to him to challenge standards. We were all over him. Then we labored at wiping all the lipstick off his face. Just then, the lights and music faded, and the live band kicked off the energy and rhythm.

# Chapter 27
## DOUGLASS

**I** was still trippin' from all the kissing—the three of them, attacking me like they had no sense. I couldn't quite read through the smile on Angel's face, wondering how she was accepting the supporting role as opposed to the superstar role she was so used to. At least she seemed comfortable now. Part of the family.

We enjoyed Will Downing, with his captivating rendition of "I Try," his duets, his new tunes, and that brilliant showmanship. I'm sitting there amid these buxom beauties, having the time of my life, having flashbacks of the good ol' days. In my mind I recalled my last TV interview with Will. It was during the hard times, when I was with Rain. When we were on access cable. I brought my newborn son along to S.O.B.'s where Will was performing. Before his show we went down to his dressing room. He held Doug Jr. while I held the camcorder, assuming the dual roles of father and TV host. Some things I'll never forget. And now, it made me happy to reciprocate, to include the balladeer in this high-energy atmosphere, the packed house giving him massive exposure.

**W**hat was intended as an intermission turned into a big ol' house party. From our vantage point, we looked on as a sea of trendy coiled crowns paraded by, beautiful auburn finger waves and coils, chic easy bobs, African Bantu twists, silky dread-locks, natural Afros, short stylish French rolls, bouf-fant curls, braided buns, Cleopatras and Oprahs, sophisticated or bouncing, owned or purchased—more heads of hair than the eye could see, bopping and swerving to deejay Kid Capri's quick-handed musical selections. Capri turned the mellow mood into a virtual dance hall, spinning classic tracks as our models strutted in time, down the aisles, along the edge of the stage, forcing the audience into a ten-minute standing ovation. Meanwhile I knew that behind the monstrous red curtain, stagehands and band members were making major adjustments, preparing for the coming of Anita.

I remained seated while my girls, and the audito-rium at large, waited anxiously, dancing out of their seats to make the best of the time. It was a helluva view. A proud sight that I was drowning in. And not just because this was such a well-attended event, but because it had indeed *been so long* since we'd seen Anita. So it was both ironic and appropriate for her to open the performance with her song "Been So Long." The audience broke into a thunderous ap-plause. And I knew that this wasn't merely a night out . . . it was a celebration.

Out of the blue, Phil had run up behind me. Something was going on. In my ear, he spoke loud enough for me to hear.

"Your lawyer's here, Doug. We got problems."

"What's up?" My eyes were still on the stage, but they were diverted by a few people down to the far side of the hall. Pointing up at us. I swore I recognized Lianne and Angel's mother.

"They've got the police with them. Something about pressing criminal charges. The lawyer talked them into letting him walk you through this . . ."

"Walk me through *what*?" I growled, my eyes meeting Phil's.

"They want you to turn yourself in."

"For what?" I blasted.

"Doug, the girl. She's still underage 'til January fifth."

I closed my eyes, not wanting to believe that this was happening. On Christmas fuckin' night. The girls were looking back at me now. At Phil, too.

"Damn, Phil. Ain't no fuckin' way I'm doin' that. *No way*."

"Doug, they're about a minute behind me. The cops, your lawyer . . . all of 'em." I looked back at Anita. She was apologizing . . .

*"I apologize . . . Honest and true . . ."*

I loved that song too. But it was time to make a move. I could almost smell the heat approaching from around the corner.

"Phil, take care of the girls. Whatever you do, don't let them take Angel. The plans don't change for tomorrow. I *will* be on vacation. By any means necessary." I was addressing Phil, but all the while I was thinking, *Lianne—the backstabber*.

"The flight info and tickets are with Deidra. I'll be waiting at the airport. Give me your house keys . . ."

Phil didn't hesitate, unsnapping the ring from his side.

"I'll reach you on the cell. Where's the limo?"

"Four doors down that way." He pointed to the lower-level exit doors. I leaned over to kiss Jo-Jo. Then Deidra. Then Angel, with a long, passionate kiss. I wanted her mother to see the kiss, in case she was still watching from the distance. But I had no time to waste.

"I gotta go."

"What's wrong?"

"Phil can fill you in. I'll see you—*all* of you—tomorrow at LaGuardia."

My heart was beating like a jazz drum riff. I looked back at Phil, knowing he'd go and stall the posse, and I grabbed the brass guardrail, swinging my body over the ledge as if I were going overboard. I dropped about fifteen feet to the carpeted aisle that ran against the wall of the auditorium. Where all of the exit doors are. The girls screamed behind me, but it was all overwhelmed by the crowd's applause. Even as Anita was about to sing her classic "Angel," I ignored the crowd of *ooh*s and *ahh*s and gasps as I strutted along the aisle, disappearing past the standing ovation and out through the side door.

# Chapter 28
## ANGEL

**A**ngelica, I want you to come with me."

I snatched my arm away and yelled, "Don't you *touch* me!" I felt myself growl and seethe. Jo-Jo and Deidra were standing across the lobby, inside of a circle, with a lawyer and some police officers, answering questions. Jo-Jo and I kept eye contact the whole time, somehow confiding in each other, knowing that they wouldn't get the best of us.

"Excuse me, officer. Am I under arrest?" I asked the flatfoot who was beside my mother—aka the bitch from hell.

"No, ma'am. But I think the lieutenant will have a few questions for you."

"Questions? Are you kidding me? I'm a superstar. If you have any questions, why don't you speak with my personal manager."

"Who's that?"

"The *bitch* right here, standing next to you."

Her hand came out of nowhere. Smacked me hard enough to turn my head half off of my shoulders. I quickly raised my hand to my cheek, huffing and puffing, trying to hold back tears.

"Don't you *ever* disrespect me like that again! As long as you live, I'll always be your mother."

The cop jumped in between us with his eyes spinning in his head. Jo-Jo ran over and embraced me. A cop ran behind her. She screamed, "Get your filthy hands offa me!"

Phil came over now. "Listen. We don't want a bigger scene than necessary. Let's just go through the motions and get out of here."

Phil probably made good sense, but honestly, I didn't feel up to the questions, the answers, the *nothin'* right now. I just wanted to get away—back to Doug, and on our vacation.

Now I saw Lianne. Once I put two and two together, I knew how all of this came about. Now it was on *for real*.

"'Scuse me, Jo-Jo, would you mind walking me to the ladies' room? I need to look at my *face*. In case she *scarred* me." I was putting on my best act, expecting the cops to lay off and have sympathy. My eyes conspired with Phil's, and Jo-Jo and I eased out of sight with no haste or aggression.


In the bathroom, Jo-Jo and I pretended to tend to my face in the mirror until a woman left. Everybody was suspect as far as we were concerned.

"What should we do?"

"If you're game."

We both looked at the window. It was half open, with the fire escape on the other side.

"What about Deidra?" I asked.

"She'll be all right. She's a big girl. Plus, Phil's with her. Right now it's about you, girl." Suddenly Lianne came into the restroom.

"Angel! Are you okay?"

Lianne rushed up in front of me. But all I did was cut into her with my eyes. Jo-Jo shoved me aside and swung on Lianne. The sucker-punch caught her right on the chin, and she kicked her too. Lianne fell back into the nearest stall, slumped on the toilet seat.

"Now, let's go."

We climbed through the window, down the fire escape, and trotted through the alley like burglars and jumped into one of the dozens of double-parked taxis out front. The luggage was already packed and waiting at the penthouse. I wasn't sure where we were vacationing; it was supposed to be a surprise. But the mission now was to get the bags and get out, in case the police decided to stake out Doug's home. I was ready to go to Egypt. *Whatever. Wherever.*

# Chapter 29
## DOUGLASS

I wasn't dreaming. And no, this wasn't the office, where phones are ringing all day and where some- one *else* usually answers them. I had to shake out of it. Both phones were ringing—my cell phone and Phil's home phone. I rubbed my forehead, then my eyes, then back around to my neck. Sleeping on Phil's couch felt comfortable at first, but there's no place like home.

"Yeah."

"Okay . . . yeah . . . wait a minute . . . Phil? Where you at?"

I had both phone lines working now. Deidra wait- ing on the cell, while I spoke to Phil.

"Cool. What about Angel? Where is she? Really*? Really!? Wow!* You think Angel hit her, or Jo-Jo? Yeah . . . I think it was her, too. She even told me about her violent past . . . scarred up some guy one day. An ex-boyfriend named Almonté. Anyway, Dei- dra's on the other line. See ya at LaGuardia. Yeah, I'll be careful. Oh, by the way, your couch sucks!"

I hung up with Phil, figuring he did the right thing staying at a friend's. The cops probably trailed him knowing that he's so close to me.

"S'up, babe? Yes . . . I'm all right. Now you've

got tickets for us all, right? So as long as Jo-Jo knows when and where to meet us, we should be cool . . . on the way to Alaska in a few hours. Don't worry. I will be on time. You be careful too. Right back atcha."

I figured things were pretty well mapped out, despite the rude awakening at the MSG. The promotion department for *SuperStar* Concerts informed me that the show finished in historic fashion. We shot quality video, the webcast went over with a record number of hits, and there was a spectacular amount of responses on the website bulletin boards. And while the website would be active with reruns and traffic throughout the holidays, the physical offices of *SuperStar* were to reopen on the 6th of January.

My tactic, in case the law wanted to get stupid, was to let 'em figure things out after the 5th, once Angel was legal.

I t was a peculiar feeling to know that all of my help, my assistants and my security, were focused on a sole concern: Angel becoming an adult. Why the forces we faced couldn't see the truth, that she was *already* an adult, and that she'd already crossed that threshold, I'll never know. Or maybe I do; maybe her mother was blaming me for the failed relationship she had with her daughter. But what they all didn't know was that, no matter how it all came about, Angel and I were meant to be. I loved that girl, regardless of my rascal ways. And I know that she's more than just another woman by my side. She's more than a platinum-selling artist, or some jailbait that I broke in. Angel was the type who empowered me. Just knowing she had my back, that she was devoted to the family, and that her career came second was all the dedication I needed to reciprocate, to forge on, and to do so relentlessly. For now, I needed to stay out of sight, away from Angel's mother. Alaska was the best idea I had yet.

I reached the airport a little early. Just paranoia I suppose. There were only a few things I could do at the airport: eat, talk on the phone, or sit and watch the CNN feed on the television monitors. Since there was time to kill, I took a seat under the closest monitor, but instead of watching TV I looked out of the window wall as flights took off down the runway. I imagined being on one of those flights, headed for Seattle, where we'd stay over for a day until we caught a connecting flight for Anchorage, Alaska. Maybe we'd take the tram and visit the Space Needle during the stopover, and in Alaska, we'd try various restaurants and taste delicious salmon and lobster until our overindulgent stomachs begged us to stop. Of course we'd stay at one of those bed & breakfast retreats and indulge some more in our own physical delicacies. And naturally, I'd impregnate Jo-Jo, Deidra, *and* Angel—one at a time or in a team effort, whatever my heart desired. Maybe we'd even stay in Alaska past the 5th of January and count the drunken Eskimos.

*Whatever. I'm crazy, I'm ready to populate the world, and last I checked, nobody was around to stop me.*

Someone was tapping me, and I woke from my

daydream. It couldn't be long until the others arrived. I turned to see who it was.

"Remember me, Mr. *SuperStar*?" And that's *all* I remembered. His face and then an immediate blackout.

# Chapter 30
## ANGEL

**M**iss? Are you okay?" said the lady, all up in my grill.

"Yeah, I'm fine. Everybody *else* is nuts around here. What right have you all got to hold me here?"

"First let me introduce myself, young lady. I'm Ms. Foster, a social worker with ACS—the Administration for Child Services."

"Well, if you didn't know, I am *not* a child."

"Please, bear with me. Can I call you Angelica?"

"That's my damn *name*." I sucked my teeth and rolled my eyes.

"I was assigned to your case because I was once in your shoes. I was also—"

"How were you *ever* in *my* shoes? Girlfriend, do you watch TV? Do you listen to the radio? Or maybe your daughters do?"

"Angelica, I'm very much aware of who you are and what you do for a living. That's why—"

"If you knew that, then you wouldn't be talking to me like I'm stupid and I wouldn't be locked in this room." I got up to bang on the door. "Hello! Hell-*ooh*! Can somebody please let me the fuck out of here?!"

"Okay. I tried to be nice. I tried. But you want to go hard, so I'll go hard." The woman was big-bodied

and seemed to be in her thirties. She got up—
lookin' able as ever—and pointed at the chair I had
been sitting in. "Now sit your BLACK ASS DOWN!
NOW!! RIGHT NOW!!"

I swear my neck must've disappeared, the way
my head sank into my shoulders and my mouth fell
open. The woman looked like she was about to haul
around and smack the shit outta me. I did what she
said. And she just might *never* have another problem
out of me. *Really.* My heart was thumpin' strong
against my breast, so much I swore I thought I saw it
moving.

"We've got a problem here, Angelica. On one
hand, there's a problem at home. I'm aware of that. I
know about the mother-daughter struggle and I'm all
too familiar with the stage-mom syndrome. On the
other hand, you're still considered a minor. And depending on what you've been through and how much
you're willing to cooperate, there may be criminal
activity involved here, including kidnapping, and
worse . . . rape.

"Now, here's what I think about you; let's start
there." Ms. Foster got up from the table and pulled
up a chair a few feet away from me. "You're a very
talented young lady, Angelica. Unfortunately, because of the frustrations at home, you've felt a need
to find comfort elsewhere. You've run into people
who you *think* love you. Listen to that—people who
you *think* love you. Now, I believe, since you're still
seventeen and this may be difficult to accept . . . that
you might be a victim . . ." The woman read me like
a book. Like I was transparent or something and she
could see right through me. I felt violated at first, but

she was so sincere. The words she said, and her authority and tact had me searchin' myself. She told me about the confidence game and how it's used to persuade young, impressionable girls. She told me about *herself*, her experiences in the streets and behind the scenes of the entertainment industry. How she had also been young and naive, and had succumbed to the thrills and impulses of a man who had money, but was manipulative and disrespectful. I tried to deny the similarities between Ms. Foster and myself. Then I tried to ignore the similarities between the men she'd come to know and the man I knew. But it wasn't easy.

She told me of the supporters who helped to lure her into the circle, and I thought of Jo-Jo and Deidra. It was all so hard to swallow, the reality thoroughly painful. I didn't know whether to give in to hurt or to be strong and fight the allegations. Cognative dissidence, Ms. Foster called it. I didn't understand; but once she explained and put her hand on my shoulder, I broke down, crying until my blouse was drenched.

I'm here for one reason, Angelica. I'm here to save your life."

Her words echoed in my head until I felt numb—a feeling I've experienced before. Ms. Foster escorted me out of A.C.S.'s Harlem facility and took me for a drive out to SISTA, a girls' home up in Orange County. It was a large property that overlooked the Hudson River. She introduced me to Adele, who gave us the grand tour. And I got to see teenage girls of all sizes and cultures involved in various activities, learning different occupations, learning about finances, about family, and how to know your true friends. They had martial arts defense courses and verbal defense courses. There was an indoor pool, tennis courts, and a gymnasium with ongoing aerobics classes and gaming. Adel explained that SISTA stood for Sistas In Stable Transition. The A, she said, stood for Academy. And I heard her nicknaming the facility *Sistacademy* a few times. We stopped in a hall where many of the girls were congregated, sounding off in a poetry forum of some kind.

"You might want to wear your sunglasses, Angel."

Ms. Foster and I stood back and listened so as not to be noticed by the others. A lot of the girls had natural, kinky blowout hairstyles. Others sported locks and a few had African Bantu twists. One girl was even bald. I noticed that no one had weaves, wigs, or even extensions. No makeup on anyone. No designer clothes or expensive jewelry. Just richly cultured young women with organic messages, projecting an effortless animal magnetism.

The young girl who was in the center of the room was already deep into her poem:

*". . . You've got to give your all*
*You've got to feel your falls*
*You've got to set your goals*
*And try your best to score . . .*

*Break the mold, go for gold,*
*Give it more, elevate and soar.*

*Tomorrow can't be promised to you today*
*You cannot pass your precious time away.*

*The more you want, the more you can achieve*
*The answer still, is that you must believe . . .*
*Keep your priorities up front and don't lose track,*
*Keep your own pace in life, proceed and don't look*
    *back."*

The group applauded the poet and she gave a humble bow before sitting back down. The next girl was heavyset and cheeky with big beautiful eyes. She was already up—anxious to present her words. The others encouraged her with applause.

"This is called 'Vapors and Fumes,'" she said.

*Vapors are fuming all around me*
*The steam is so thick, I can't hardly see*
*Anger and stress flowing like a breeze*
*Something's got to give, gotta set me free*
*Different girls and their ways, milling around,*
*If they don't say a word, still I hear their*
    *sounds . . .*
*Like the girl's beating heart, or the drowning pulse*
*The blood siphons everywhere without remorse.*

*I try to stay calm and ignore it all*
*But something always nears, I can hear it call*
*Trouble just lurking round here and there*
*And a strict code of silence still fills the air*

*You can't hear him banging inside of my walls*
*I still want to kill him—if only he calls*

*He's a sinister being in my crack and my curve*
*I don't know how he got here—where he got the*
    *nerve . . .*

*I want to be a wife, and I want to have kids*
*But I keep asking God, What I s'pose t' done*
    *did?*
*And I can't help remembering my very best*
    *friends*
*I thought they'd stick by me, but they just pretend*

*I still think of things I'll do once I'm home*
*I let my mind wander, I let my mind roam*
*I dream of the moon, and other great unknowns*
*Other times I'm thankful just to be all alone*

*Vapors are fuming all over me*
*The steam is so thick, I can hardly see*
*Anger and stress flowing like a breeze*
*Something's got to give, gotta set me free*

Everybody stood up and applauded. Ms. Foster
and I clapped too.

"Wow," I said, eye-to-eye with the social worker.

Then Adele said in a low voice, "She was gang-
raped. Went after her attackers afterward and killed
one. This is all therapeutic for her."

As I watched a few girls hugging the latest presenter, I couldn't help but lose it myself. Tears fell
and my body gravitated toward Ms. Foster's. I embraced her with sniffles and sobs. That's when the
others noticed us. One girl screamed and seemed to
shake uncontrollably. Another girl tried to calm her,

and now the word spread: A celebrity was in the room. I heard my name working its way around, and now everyone was in my face.

"Why don't you say something to the girls, Angelica? I'm sure they'd appreciate it."

Ms. Foster's words helped to ease my sudden stage fright. I wiped away my tears, embarrassed, yet buried down deep inside me was a growing confidence that I had not forgotten. I faltered at first, but found my way through the few dozen girls. Holding hands. Giving hugs. Feeling wonderful. I reached the heavyset girl who wrote the "Vapors" poem and gave her the warmest, heartiest hug I could muster.

"Your poem touched my heart. Thank you."

"Thank you, too." The girl's voice seemed to fade.

Another girl asked, "Can you sing a song?"

"Yeah, can you?" said another.

"Angel! Angel! Angel! Angel!" they all began to chant. I didn't realize how loved I was. I looked back at Ms. Foster for help here. Her smile was a proud one. Meanwhile, Adele maintained crowd control.

"Thank you. Thank you from the bottom of my heart. You've given me such a warm welcome, just when I needed it. I would like to sing a song. It's one I wrote for my next album—whenever I get around to that—and I'd like to dedicate it to all of you. To my girls at Sistacademy. It's called 'My Dream.'

*If I could live forever*
*Could I ever change a thing?*

*Could the seasons change from summertime to*
*   spring?*

*Could I end the greed and hunger?*
*Could I keep the family strong?*
*Could I learn to go through life and get along?*
*It may not be real*
*But my vision justifies the way I feel*
*If I could live forever in my dreams then would*
*   you come with me?*

*If patience is a virtue*
*Then can pleasure lead the way?*
*And can everyone's potential be the same?*

*And if peace on earth in music*
*Brought us peace on earth in life,*
*Could my dream go on beyond my thoughts*
*   tonight?*

I choked up. Couldn't sing the rest. So I spoke . . .

*I know that my dream*
*is the way that life should be . . .*
*or so it seems . . .*

*and since dreams can last a lifetime,*
*then I might . . . close my eyes and dream*
*this dream of mine . . . for life . . .*

The silence was haunting, even in the daylight.
There were sniffles. Then a clap. Then a progression
of claps, building to large applause.

I took a bow. Smiling through my own tears. Addressing girls who ran up to hug me. I signed autographs and answered questions.

The entire experience was breathtaking and unforgettable.

# Chapter 31
## DOUGLASS

I woke up looking up at a white ceiling in a hospital room somewhere in Queens. A cop was sitting over in the corner, flipping through some back issues of *Newsweek* magazine. I raised my head and back from the bed when I realized my wrist was cuffed to the bed guard on my left.

"Son-of-a . . ."

"Relax, dude. You're being detained until the doc gives you a clean bill o' health. Then it's over ta central bookin' fa ya."

I could see he was but a peon and that talking to him would be fruitless. I was left to just flop back on the pillow. I thought back to the last thing I remembered seeing: Nitro. A blind shot to my head. A sharp pain.

"OUCH!" The pain came back. It was throbbing now. A splitting headache. I wanted to be unconscious again. To escape the pain.

The cop had a spent coffee cup and a crumpled wax bag from Dunkin' Donuts. I was suddenly hungry. A nurse came in to check my temperature. The clock on the wall said it was close to six in the evening. Pills. A cup of dry-ass water.

"You hungry, sir?" *No. I'm eating oxygen for dinner. Of course I'm hungry, bitch.*

"Yes, ma'am. Anything good on the menu?"

She didn't answer, but chuckled under her breath. So did the cop. Maybe I'd be getting bread and water, I thought, as the nurse left the room.

"Six o'clock news—never miss it. Hope you don't mind," said the cop.

And I did mind, but I was hurting. My head was killing me. I was in no shape to argue. Besides, he didn't look like he was gonna take no for an answer.

He flipped around until he landed on channel five. Their familiar music intro and graphics preceded the appearance of the newscasting duo.

"It's ten below zero and snowing heavily on this Sunday evening. Thank you for joining us." The female cut in now and the camera shot changed to an upper body image of her. A square appeared to her side with a recent photo of Angel. The words "ANGEL'S RESCUE" were superimposed over the bottom of the picture.

"Good evening, New York. Wonderful news tonight. The superstar singer-actress Angel is back in the custody of her guardians tonight, after what her mother claims has been a month-long fight for her soul. Authorities have since arrested this man, twenty-seven-year-old Douglass Grey, owner-proprietor of the entertainment empire known as SuperStar Communications . . ."

*Now, I've heard everything,* I told myself.

"Hey, that's you. Damn, dude, you're a *star*!" The cop was being sarcastic and I wished I could put a foot in his ass.

The story went on for another few minutes, with footage of my TV shows, my offices, the magazine, and some of the holiday extravaganza I promoted. They even showed clips of Anita Baker and Will Downing, twisting those innocent parties all up in *my* mess. SHIT! I thought I'd never hear the end of this as I watched what felt like endless clips from Angel's various TV appearances, shots of her with the president, onstage at Disney, at the Grammys, the Teen Choice Awards, the People's Choice Awards, and even her work on Sesame Street and in commercials as a child. To top that, I almost choked when Lianne came on, confirming shit, all the allegations made against me, as if she was an official of some kind.

This all painted Angel's moms as the innocent one in the equation. As pure as cotton.

Kara and Veronica did interviews as well, adding to Angel's glow as the world's "good girl." The final image was the fusion of Angel and I, side by side with a rip down the middle. As if we broke up. The newscasters shook their heads, with expressions that evidenced a near miss, and promised more details from the current investigation as they were made available.

With my head back against the pillow and the cop blabbing on about how I "done a bad, bad thing," I peered out of the window at the snowflakes. It was the only solid grip I had on reality until I fell asleep to create my own. The next thing I knew, I was being taken down the corridor, bed and all, past the nurse's station and into a waiting elevator. Two officers stood guard while two hospital orderlies navigated, snickering the whole time, like they knew something that I didn't. Once we were in the basement, I began to get nervous, as the bed was pushed down dark halls with only glowing exit signs to set the course.

"Where are you taking—" My mouth was muffled, with one of the cop's palms pressing against my face. I couldn't see which one, but I strained myself trying. There was finally light ahead, with another cop near a doorway, waiting. I could see the cop now—the one with the greasy palm against my lips. It was Nitro in a uniform. Things were looking mighty shady with every passing second.

Now the lights nearly blinded me. I lifted my free hand to cover my eyes, but just as fast, my wrist was grabbed. And now that one was cuffed to the opposite bed guard. I had to close my eyes to keep my head from spinning. But that didn't matter; once the bed stopped moving, duct tape was affixed to my eyes and mouth. I couldn't speak. I couldn't see. Water was dripping somewhere. A motor hummed in the distance. The soft fizzing must be coming from all the bright lights around. Rubber gloves snapped. Then again. And again. Silverware? Tools?

Metal was clinking and clanking. Something ripped, like leather. Yes, leather . . . with buckles. Suddenly my legs were strapped down to the far ends of the bed. My body was restrained, and two of those gloved hands were pulling my head back. And now some type of harness was fixed over my head and face so my head lay stiff. There was more ripping, only this was from my clothes. My pants were cut to shreds, I could feel a cool breeze about my upper thighs and groin. Now a strap was placed over my midsection, pulled so tight that my waist was pinned from even the slightest amount of slack. I trembled.

I sensed that there were close to a half dozen people around me, looking at me in my ripped clothes. Yet they hadn't said a word. *At least they left my underwear on,* I thought. But now those were pulled off too. My rectum immediately contracted. I wondered why all my other clothes were left on—while only there, around my dick, was exposed.

"Hello, Douglass." The female voice sounded familiar. "Do you know who this is?" I didn't. "Oh, that's right. You can't speak now, can you? Well, raise one finger for yes . . . two for no."

My hand was lying by my side, palm to the mattress. I raised two fingers.

"Hmmm, well, let me give you a hint. You gave me a five on your list of sex partners." She was laughing now, that hearty, husky laugh that means someone's got the upper hand. It took less than ten seconds before I was hyperventilating under the tape. It was her. But how? When? Why?

I flipped through all of my intelligences, wondering how my ex-girlfriend . . . how Rain got me in this position. Were cops *working* for her? Was *she* a cop now? Was she working at the hospital? Then I questioned myself, asking if I had ever done anything so bad to her to deserve such torture. The buzzing began. The same sound I hear when Rob cuts my hair. I moaned under the tape over my mouth. I sobbed under the tape over my eyes. I whined for mercy and tried to make out words, becoming more and more desperate.

My breathing was exhausted.

"Don't worry, playboy. This'll hurt at first. But in time the pain will be excruciating enough that you'll lose consciousness. We'll leave the wound open so that the blood will continue to run. Hopefully this all won't take more than two hours."

These words caused me to heave, followed by a stint of persistent coughs. The buzzing came closer—close enough for me to feel a vibration and then a sharp blade severing my penis. I screamed, "YOU'RE CUTTING MY DICK OFF!!!" at the top of my lungs. Laughter now.

I could make out images all of a sudden. The hospital room again. The same cop. Cracking up.

"No. They didn't start that yet. The judge will need to see you first. Then maybe you'll get it cut off. They do that to you guys lately, cuttin' 'em off. You lose your libido I hear."

He broke up. Killing himself with his jokes. I even had to consider if he might be telling the truth. Still, there was relief. I could see the snow again. Never a more pleasant sight. It had been a most horrible dream.

My heart seemed to take forever to resume beating at its normal tempo. And as hard as I was breathing, with that cyclone tossing around inside of my head, I should've had a heart attack. But instead, I laid back with my eyes still searching outside of the window. I was numb as could be.

Thinking . . . questioning . . . I was scared for my-

self. Indeed I had problems. I recognized not only
my dysfunctional past, but how I'd snowballed into
a demon. I couldn't cry anymore. Ran out of tears.
God, how I needed help.

By 11 P.M., it was just me, the flickering glow
from the monitor, and the sleeping, snoring top cop.
It wasn't the draft, but the light from out in the hallway that made me turn my head. I saw the usual outline of the nurse in her outfit and what I assumed
was a doctor behind her. I didn't bother to look
twice. I just turned my head back toward the snow.

"Shhh . . ." I heard the whisper and saw her finger,
vertical against her lips. I couldn't believe my eyes,
guessing that I was hallucinating again. But it sure
was Jo-Jo disguised as a nurse. I immediately turned
toward the cop. Still asleep. A man was standing
with his back to me, facing the cop. From his pocket
he pulled out a small glass vial with clear solution in
it. He opened it and shook it into a handful of gauze.
Now he had the gauze pressed to the cop's nose and
mouth, while harnessing his body—controlling him
with a knee to the chest and a firm grip on his arm.
Clearly, he was no doctor. I eventually made out that
it was Phil disabling the cop. My people were rescu-
ing me.

# Chapter 32
## ANGEL

I stayed with Ms. Foster. She had a first-floor apartment in a brownstone on West 126th Street, close to a school and the backstage door of the Apollo Theater. I also learned that she was a powerful woman in the Harlem community, that she's been a savior of young ethnic girls for years. A leader and an activist. Ms. Foster took part in many of the community's social concerns. And she was a board member for a few organizations that maintained a strong foothold in the advancement of the poor and underprivileged.

For two days I was humbled and speechless, gazing at the plaques on her wall, and the framed articles about her. There were photo albums too numerous to keep on one shelf. And there was me, in awe of all that I saw, all that I'd experienced in Ms. Foster's presence. She treated me better than a celebrity; not with the here-today-gone-tomorrow attitude, always expecting the next one to come along. No. I was Angelica next to Ms. Foster. I was a black woman. I was human. It was these times that gave me an opportunity to reflect upon how fast I'd grown in such a short time, missing out on the finer things in life: compassion, humility, and the understanding of what my contribution would be during my short stay on the earth. What was my purpose?

I had to rethink my status as a singer, the folks I'd associated with, and the negative messages and images I was exposed to. My mother pushed my potential for all the wrong reasons. To Douglass I was just another piece on his chessboard . . . maybe even a pawn. Of that I wasn't sure. I had to redefine who the world was seeing when they watched or heard Angel. I had to do what mattered for me. It wasn't about recording songs, going platinum, or television appearances. It was about life. About destiny. About me.

"The Harlem Chamber of Commerce is putting on a benefit concert at the Apollo on New Year's Eve. Part of the proceeds will benefit Hale House."

"I've been there, Ms. Foster. I've seen the children."

"The other beneficiary is Sistacademy. Would you like to go with me?"

"Really? I'd love to. Do you think I can sing a song, help out in some way?"

"Now, why didn't I think of that?" She smiled, then asked, "Do you think you can sing the one about your dream? The one you sang up at Sistacademy?"

"Anything you ask, Ms. Foster. Anything at all. I just hope I can sing the whole song this time."

On New Year's Eve, 126th Street was a very different atmosphere from how it looks normally. Trailers lined both sides of the street, allowing no through traffic to pass. The ends of the block were barricaded and policed, only permitting access to performers, their handlers, and theater personnel. Scores of folks who moved back and forth between trailers and in and out of the theater's stage entrance were immediately distinguishable by fluorescent, star-shaped laminates.

Generators hummed all over the place, powering the remote vehicles and keeping those inside nice and warm. Meanwhile, I stayed with Adele and the group of girls I met up at Sistacademy. We had a trailer all to ourselves, because a few of the girls were due to present their spoken word talents. Visitors stopped in throughout the night to take photos and to sign autographs for the girls. I helped Adele to keep the girls orderly and cordial in the presence of the celebrities, politicians, and community leaders who visited. I helped to serve refreshments, and acted as a one-woman audience for them as they rehearsed their poems. I was laboring so much, I set my usual pre-stage rituals aside just to help everyone else. Ms. Foster had been going in and out of the trailer all evening— dutifully troubleshooting so that the dozens of guest performers, the audience, and her legion of volunteers would proceed under the most favorable circumstances. It was only now that she realized I was sweating like a turkey during open season.

"Angelica? Don't you think you're overworking yourself? You know, the show's gonna start soon." She was stepping up into the trailer again.

"No, it's okay, Ms. Foster. I just wanna make things right for the girls . . ."

"Yeah. And soon she'll be putting me out of a job," said Adele. Ms. Foster wagged her head.

"Well, I have a visitor outside who'd like to see you."

"No problem. Who is it? Let 'em in."

"Ma'am?" Ms. Foster turned to address the person and stepped aside as Kara came up into the trailer.

"Kara!" I shrieked excitedly. "Omigosh!" Now the whole trailer was alerted, many jumping to their feet enthusiastically, congregating around the two of us as we embraced like long-lost pals.

"Where have you been? I've tried to call you; left you messages at home, on your voice mail . . ." I pushed away a tear before answering her. Ms. Foster urged the others to give us room.

"I haven't been home in a long time, Kara. It's . . . it's a long story. A very long story."

"They said you were performing tonight."

"Uh-hmmm."

"Like *this*, baby? You can't go out there like *this*. Your *image* . . . you've got an image to uphold, girl. But I shouldn't have to tell you about that."

"I wish I had an image. I really do. But the way things have been spinning around here, I sometimes don't know who I am anymore."

"Okay, listen, I don't know what's been going on with you . . . but I'll be damned if I'm gonna let you play yourself out there in front of the Apollo audience. You not goin' out there all tore up; they'll rip you to shreds before you get to sing one note."

I was speechless, dropping my eyes to the trailer floor. Kara turned to consult with Ms. Foster. I overheard her saying something about a dressing room inside the theater. Then Kara took my hand. Ms. Foster nodded to me. I let Kara lead me out of the

SEEMS LIKE YOU'RE READY 253

trailer, stepping over a series of cables snaking about the pavement, and then across the street into the stage door. I noticed her pull out an all-access pass for the doorman to see.

"Don't be silly, Ms. Kara. You know *you* don't need to show me that." Sweet old fogy.

"Thanks. She's with me," Kara mentioned as we strutted over the threshold. Kara, the shepherd.

"You have a dressing room here?"

"I have a dressing room here . . . a permanent one." Nothing surprised me now. Kara escorted me up a flight of steps, while explaining what I didn't know.

"See, there're a few dozen dressing rooms here on . . . well, I don't even know *how* many floors . . . They've named the rooms after notable Apollo legends. But there were others that they sold leases to. So, if I'm hosting a show here, I can make myself at home in a dressing room that's set up for me."

We stepped into the swankiest dressing room I'd ever been in. Almost all white and stately.

"Of course, because I *do* lease a dressing room here, it gives me a little pull with the foundation, so they look out for me on bookings. I host like half of the stuff that plays here . . . depending on my movie schedule."

"What about the modeling? How do you have time?"

"Oh, a lot of my work, meetings and stuff, takes place here in New York, so I figured it wouldn't hurt to stay in touch with my people. You know, come and host a show or so a week. It's good exposure, too. I can set an example for other aspiring models and actresses from the inner city. I ain't gonna be pretty forever, babe. Gotta face that." Kara walked across the carpet, past a plush leather couch and the glistening vanity. "Now, this is what I want you to see." She pulled open a sliding door to a closet before she cried out, "Ta-*daaah!*"

"Ohhh-*kay*. Now you're talkin'. They gave you this stuff?" I gazed at the incredible wardrobe.

"'Course not, silly. I mean . . . we're talkin' the Apollo here, girl, not the Ritz. This is from the designers I work with. Calvin, Donna Karan, Prada, Versace. It never seems to end. Take your pick."

"You're kidding. Kara—no."

"Come on, Angel. I have a midtown apartment full of this stuff. If I gave you half of it I wouldn't notice . . ."

She stepped to her right, pointing things out like a salesperson would, urging me to make myself at home.

"The shower is that way," she said, pointing like a traffic cop. I got the message loud and clear.

The shower was nice. I chose a conservative outfit— a bit of street, a bit of glamour. Burgundy and white. A cowgirl hat to match the leather pants? *Nahh.*

"The show's starting, girl." Kara came over to give me a sweet kiss on the cheek, then rubbed off the lipstick. Her assistant opened the door.

"Kara, one minute, thirty seconds."

"I'll send Brenda up to let you know your cue," Kara said to me. "Good luck. I'll be cheering for you." And Kara was gone just like that.

I felt like a princess there in her dressing room. As if nothing in the world was wrong and everything

was right. I sat at the vanity and looked through a se-
lection of thirty lip glosses. I went with purple rose
and made my lips shine too. I blew a kiss, intrigued
at how easy it was to impress myself . . . how easy it
was to remember myself here, in the lap of luxury,
in some other dressing room at a Hollywood studio,
or in a green room before an interview, or backstage
at an awards show. It felt so easy to get caught up,
fixated on the fame that called out to me. It was at
that moment when I decided it was my right.

Ms. Foster told me a lot about talent, hard work,
and self-consciousness. But I figured I was merely
missing the self-consciousness in my life, 'cause all
I've known is my talent and how to work hard. It
was something I actually *loved* to do.

I heard a knock at the door. I figured Brenda was
ready for me, so I ran up to open it.

"Hi." He was leaning on the doorjamb. Cool as
Denzel or Billy Dee. Hands in his pockets. That
smile that I fell for . . . the one my mother fell for . . .
the one the world knew as Sincere. I immediately
slammed the door on him, but his foot was there.
Then I leaned my body against it.

"I swear—I'll scream. I *swear*!" But he pushed
his way in and closed the door behind him.

"Come on, Angel. What are you gonna scream
for? And who's coming? The old man at the back
door? Kara? She's already onstage."

I screamed anyway, recalling Roscoe's and how
this man who I thought was the dream date turned
out to be my worst nightmare. And worse than that
was how this man (since he was a singer) was likely

to show up at any large event I was a part of. And the Apollo wasn't even on my schedule! It seemed that Sincere would always have as much access as God, and that would continue to haunt me as long as I didn't do anything about it. And so, I screamed again. To think I just came from the shower, still with a towel on, and I wasn't safe! I didn't care who did or didn't hear me. He wouldn't get access to me! When I screamed again I guess it concerned him, and he rushed me and gripped my mouth. I couldn't bite him, couldn't yell, couldn't nothin'. Now he was behind me, the other arm around my arms and waist.

In my ear now, he said, "Now, Angel, is that the way to treat an old friend?"

*Friend? You're an asshole.*

"And did you think you'd get away from me so easy?"

He kissed me on the cheek, all nasty, his tongue lickin' me. I could feel him behind me with his stiff bulge at the small of my back. For an instant I almost fell limp. I almost gave up and fainted in his arms. Then I thought of Ms. Foster and her strength. I thought of Myra, the heavyset girl who was gang-raped. I had to be strong. I noticed the dressing room door hadn't closed all the way.

*Hadn't anyone heard me scream?* I wondered.

And now I saw movement beyond the door, maybe someone heading up the stairs. My instincts kicked in and I stomped on Sincere's left toe. He yelled and immediately let go, grabbing his foot. I screamed again.

# Chapter 33
## DOUGLASS

**W**hen I heared the scream, I hurried to push open the door. It sounded genuine . . . too much like Angel to be the television. That sucker-ass singer from NUBIAN was grabbing his foot, hopping around like he got shot.

"Doug!" Angel yelled. But her call for me seemed twisted, stuck somewhere between relief and fear.

"You all right?"

"He attacked me!" she shouted.

*Fuck it*, I thought. And I rushed him. Charged his ass until he fell back into the vanity, crashing the mirror along with it. He was awkward now, half slumped against the vanity. But it was the perfect position for me to go to his body. I snapped.

Left hook. Right hook. Left uppercut. Right cross. He never had a chance to return a punch, and one of my shots sent him traveling farther into the vanity. All of the makeup and the broken mirror—lightbulbs and all—fell to the floor. There was some blood, and I briefly felt sorry for somebody's white carpet.

When I was sure that the threat was gone, I turned to find Angel heading for the door. But I hurried to grab her arm. I had to feel her. Had to say what I had to say.

"Angel, *Angel*, where you goin'? Baby, it's me, Douglass. It's all right."

She seemed confused. Still frightened. Something was wrong. I could feel it. Jo-Jo told me that she and Angel were intercepted at my penthouse. That she was taken by some social worker. So then how had she managed to get here? My mind calculated so many variables—the benefit, some community activists who had organized the event . . . I wanted to ask her, but instead I started talking. It's what makes me feel better, in control of everything. Of *myself*. Slowly and in an unthreatening way, I closed the door.

"Angel, you're wearing a towel! Where are you going? Please, hear me out. I need to come clean with you . . ." I had to swallow. It's been awhile—if ever—that I gave testimony. "Please, have a seat. *Please*."

Angel finally sank into the cushy couch and began to pull on clothes while I was left standing, superior as usual. But that wasn't my intention. I wanted all along to spill myself in her lap. I inevitably kneeled. I *wanted* to feel lower than her. I needed to.

"Angel, you're looking at a growing young man. I say young because, in a way, I have a lot of learning to do. But in fact, I'm gonna be twenty-eight years old soon. Please hear me out . . ."

Angel's eyes were buggin'. Like she was in a stupor.

"When I met you, we had a sincere conversation. It started as an interview. But it turned into a chat between two human beings. Me—a man. You—the woman. I'm vulnerable when it comes to beauty;

and you're naturally beautiful. When I see beauty, if it comes within my reach, I've always been the one to reach out and grab it. I just gotta have it. Call it a sickness. Call it what you want. But it *calls* me. It shouts at me. You pulled me in with sheer animal magnetism. And I acted naturally. I followed my heart. I wanted to touch you, to meet you, and to be melted by you. I turned on the charm as best I could, and the only way I knew how."

"And I fell for it."

"Yeah, but why is that so bad? Why can't it just be what it is? If we were worms or flies or cats, would it matter? Would it? We might not even have names, but we'd be lovin' each other up . . ."

I went on to say, "And this idea of *rape*, and taking advantage of a minor—*please*! You are old enough according to Virginia laws. In other countries you're of age. So just because we're in the United fuckin' States, what we did is supposed to be illegal? Immoral? Unethical? Shit, I was in love with your body. I was in love with your mind. I was in love with you, Angel, despite being with Jo-Jo and Deidra . . ."

Angel inhaled. Her eyes widening at the truth I'd just shared.

"Yes. Yes, Angel, we're all partners. And there are a couple of others that I— Well, the point is now you know. But . . ." I tried to hold her hand. She jerked it away. ". . . aside from that, things don't change. What we had, or *have*, is true indeed. That's what *is*. Don't hate me because I like abundance or because I don't seem to have a limit. If that's my being a twisted sonofabitch, well, then so be it. Maybe that's just not *for* you. But don't hurt me. Don't lock me away because I followed my heart. I loved you the best way I knew how. With lust, passion, and intensity." Now I was crying. My head in her lap and hands at her sides. My voice muffled, I continued on, saying, "All I want is to love and be loved. No limits . . . no limits." I sobbed, pleading for my life. "I'm sorry if I've hurt you in some way. But you never showed me you were hurt. You wanted it too . . . you wanted it too . . ."

There in her lap. I was the player turned bitch. I was a mess. And then our moment of silence was broken by Sincere's moan, as he tried to raise up from the destroyed vanity.

"Douglass, I believe you. I believe you. I've never had a man cry in my lap—that's for sure." She took a deep breath. Her hands on my arms and then petting my head.

"Baby . . . baby . . ." She leaned down to kiss my head. "I need some time to think. Plus . . ." The door eased open. One of the stagehands was standing there, her mouth open.

"Uhm . . . sixty seconds?" said the stagehand.

I nodded, looking over at Sincere, struggling out of his brief coma.

"Oh, him? He'll be aiight," Angel told the stagehand with a flick of her hand. Meanwhile, she quickly pulled on the rest of her outfit. "I'm coming now, Brenda. I'm coming."

I was on my feet again, wiping the tears from my own face. I was somewhat helpless watching Angel rush to get ready. But I had no problem helping Sincere up and out of the dressing room.

"I've gotta do a song. I don't think you should wait here."

"Then—what? Do you wanna get together after the show?"

"I don't know. I don't know . . ." She left to catch up with Brenda. I got up, lost somewhere between a bad dream and a nightmare.

"Angel," I shouted, and ran behind her. She was already halfway down the steps. "Angel." My hand was on her shoulder. I moved in to steal a kiss. She sighed—that want for escape, that disagreeable sound, passing from her mouth into mine. Then she submitted, hungry for me as well. It was a confused, tension-filled kiss.

"I gotta go," she said, ripping her lips from mine.

Then she was gone. I was slow behind her, telling myself the things I didn't tell her; that I was guilty for my foul mouth and for my foul thoughts. I wanted to unveil my whole painful life to her. Sometimes you just never get to say it all.

The steps from the dressing rooms descend to a point just shy of the Apollo backstage area. It's dark, busy, and buzzing with energy. I could hear Kara out onstage. Her voice projecting out into a standing-room-only crowd. James and I acknowledged one another. He's been the stage manager at the Apollo for years. I winked at him, essentially thanking him for the full-access passes. I took a side door, which opened to the main auditorium.

"And now, ladies and gentlemen, the moment you've been waiting for. She's a triple-platinum-selling artist, she's the star of the hit TV show *AN-*

*GELIQUE*, and now, she's set to be a supermodel too. There's no end in sight for her talents. Please give a warm round of applause to . . . ANGEL!"

I strolled up the aisle to get a better view as Angel came out onstage. The crowd was on their feet before she said a word.

"Thank you. Thank you very much. I was asked to sing a certain song tonight, but, well . . . I've decided on another. This is called 'If You Won't Wait' and I wrote it just the other day. You may recognize the music because the track is from another song. However, the lyrics are my own, and they're very special. I dedicate this to my friend."

I was at the back of the auditorium now, able to see after everyone was seated.

*"Lust versus love,*
*It's a choice we must make,*
*Or do we search the universe*
*For that one true soul mate . . .*

*Conflicts unresolved*
*Confusion in our hearts*
*So many good intentions*
*So easily fall apart*

*Separation and deviation*
*The walls that truth cannot climb*
*The force that pulls us apart*
*The ways we hate with our hearts*

*It's the distance in our desires*
*That can leave both of us blind*

*Lack of patience and time wasted,*
*A memory we will never again find*

*If your faith is not strong*
*Then it's time you moved on*
*Swallow your pride, make up your mind*
*'Cause this could be all wrong."*

I listened closely as the words penetrated me to the bone. Separation and deviation. Swallow your pride. I was reading between the lines. She was singing about me. About *us*. And now, she was singing the chorus to the song.

*"If you won't wait for me*
*I'll have to say it's okay*
*'Cause when the day ends*
*More love will come my way . . .*

*If you won't wait for me*
*Then so be it, just go*
*You'll live a new life*
*A new world to explore."*

She wanted me to wait, I figured. And if I don't, then she'd look somewhere else. Wow. Now she was looking dead at me. I could tell.

*"All of those yesterdays*
*Keep my mind occupied*
*Last time I held you close to my body*
*It was as close as being inside*

*We made lovin' like the novels say*

*We brought in the sun and moon*
*How could life torture*
*And separate me from you . . . from you . . .*

*If you want me, then you'd show me*
*And if you needed me like before,*
*Then I could stand all the pain,*
*And all the waiting in vain*

*These sad emotions I could endure . . .*
*But these tensions, I should mention*
*They've reached a point of no return . . .*
*So while the smoke is still clear,*
*and since your place is not here*
*mark this down . . . lesson learned."*

All I could say was *whoa*. She was obviously
sending me a message. Right to my heart. She was
still, as the audience rose to its feet once again, absorbed in the emotions that she relayed in her words.
I felt myself swallow. Maybe it was my pride. But I
knew it was over, at least for now. I couldn't stay
here any longer since I was now a "wanted man." I
could only hope that Angel would help rectify that
over the coming days, regardless of what her mother
urged. But for the time being, I put my hand to my
lips and then turned it toward her. She did the same
at the close of her performance. And nobody would
ever know that we just said good-bye. Nobody but
my Angel and I.